These stories are works of fiction. Names, characters, places, and incidents are fictitious and any similarities to actual persons, locations, or events is coincidental.

ISBN: 978-1-989206-81-2

Cover image created over *Portrait of Ludwig Van Beethoven* by Joseph Karl Stieler, 1820 (Joseph Karl Stieler 1781-1858)

SLIGHTLY OFF-CENTER

SAM W. ANDERSON

"Sam W. Anderson establishes himself as a neo-pulp pioneer with this collection of opium dreams. Filled with the type of violence and psychosis that makes our country great, *Slightly Off-Center* is a hell of a lot more than slightly entertaining. One thing is certain: we need more dark and twisted minds like Anderson's."

–Jon Bassoff, author of
Captain Clive's Dreamworld

"In Sam W. Anderson's new collection *Slightly Off-Center* we encounter everything from red necks and talking dogs to supernatural iPhones and oversexed hoodlums in mashups of pulp horror, science fiction, and crime with Anderson's unique and compelling narrative spin. This is noir fiction renewed with heavy doses of humor and the author's keen ear for the grim poetry available in everyday conversation."

–Steve Rasnic Tem, author *of Figures Unseen:*
Selected Stories and *Thanatrauma: Stories*
(Valancourt Books)

"It's Sam W. Anderson at his least sane! A dark, disturbing, and consistently excellent collection of very, very weird stories.

–Jeff Strand, author of
Candy Coated Madness

"Get ready to have your mind folded, spindled and mutilated by Sam W. Anderson. His formidable imagination is on full display in these exhilarating tales of the weird, the dangerous, and the offbeat. OFF CENTER is a captivating showcase of Anderson's sizable talent, and I strongly recommend it."

–Ray Garton, author of
Live Girls and *Ravenous*

"Don't let the title fool you...there is *nothing* Off Center about these stories. They hit the mark each time – between the eyes, straight through the heart...and sometimes a bit lower."

–P.D. Cacek, Stoker-winning author of
Second Lives and *Second Chances*

"If there were any doubts Sam W. Anderson had one of the finest imaginations of any working writer, the stories in this aptly titled collection should obliterate them. Original, deft, and always slightly off center, this collection is a rogue's gallery of imaginative tales that slip through time and genre to create a deeply unnerving reading experience."

–Hank Early, author of
the Earl Marcus mysteries

SLIGHTLY OFF-CENTER

SON OF...A BITCH

JUSTAFACEINTHECROWD.COM, INC.

HATE CRIMES AND THERAPY OVER CREAMED CHIPPED BEEF

ON YOU; IN YOU

THE MADAM IN ROOM 217

DEAD QUIET

CONTINUATION 2020

THE GIRL FROM THE END OF THE BAR

YAKUZA PRINCESS

THE FINAL EDITION OF THE EAST PRAIRIE RECORDER

IF MAMA AIN'T HAPPY

DISH TIME

SON OF...A BITCH

"C'mon, Dave, give me a steak already."

The cheapskate pretends not to hear and focuses on his grill. If he thinks I'm going to shut up for some hamburger, he best think again—but that'd probably tax his puny brain. Of all the possible people here in Yonkers, I get stuck with Dave as the only one who can understand me. He's just a lousy postal worker, sworn enemy of any self-respecting creature. A butcher, now that would have been nice.

"I said give me a fucking steak."

"You know, I'm shocked to hear dogs have such foul mouths. Especially, a black lab. You seem so nice."

"Fuck you." I lift my leg on the chain-link fence separating our yards. "Have you listened to us bark, Dave? Do we sound like we're singing ballads and lullabies? Pretty much everything we say is yelling because you're too self-absorbed to listen."

I shouldn't be so hard on the guy, but it's too damn hot to care. I can't remember a New York summer this miserable, and all I have is this warm water full of dead ants and grass clippings. I'd rip out somebody's throat for some of that cold stuff in the big bowl in the bathroom. Damn, that's some tasty water.

Dave stands on his small patio and flips the meat. Definitely hamburger. He looks even more pathetic than usual with his cut-off shorts and pasty legs. He bobs his head to the beat of music blaring from his house—some disco song sung by a duck. Humans are weird.

I'm ready to walk away when I spy Cat at the pet door. I hate Cat. Damn thing gives me the creeps with its slitted eyes and nine lives. That's simply not natural. I turn back—hamburger's plenty fine, anyway.

"You thought about our earlier talk?" I ask. He tosses a patty over the fence, and I catch it. In two bites, it's gone. Fuck, I love hamburger!

"How could I not?" he says. "A guy hears the neighbor's dog talking at him, it kind of stays fresh in the mind." Dave smiles, like he's said something of value.

Looking at his goofy grin, I almost feel sorry for the putz. He's dumpy and quiet, and I've never seen any of the good-smelling ones come to his house. His hair is like a Brillo pad. I've chewed up one before—they break apart and get stuck in your teeth. Taste like shit, too. Was in no way worth the beating I got.

"Are you going to do it?"

"C'mon, Harvey, be serious."

"Dave, you're talking to a dog, and I'm the one that's supposed to be serious?" Of course, I'm talking to this pea brain, so...

As he bites into his hamburger, ketchup squeezes out down the front of his undersized t-shirt. It looks like blood across the yellow happy face printed on front. It also looks delicious.

"Sorry, Harv." Another bite, and more ketchup escapes. I salivate. I smell another patty on the grill and hope it's got my name on it. "I don't believe any of this," he says, still chewing. "I ain't going to do it."

I'm almost relieved. The whole idea seems idiotic, anyway, but I can't let it go without trying one more time. Cat's right here watching, and I'd never hear the end of it. In my nicest bark I say, "Come here, Dave,"

"You're not going to pee on my shoes again? These are some brand-new Traxx."

"Nah, that's only funny the first time." But, damn, is it funny. "I just want to talk. You know—canine to man."

From two blocks over, I hear Ginger barking at me to "leave that poor guy alone." If she hadn't had gotten fixed two months ago, I may have listened to her. That schnauzer snatch holds no power over me anymore.

Dave ambles closer, the scent of ketchup and hamburger grease grows stronger. He crouches by the fence, and sweat pours off him. "Okay, what do you want, Harvey?"

"I thought you said you don't believe any of this shit."

"Yeah...and?"

"Then why'd you come over here? You must think I'm talking to you, right?"

Dave stands. As he searches for a philosophical argument to counter, I lift my leg and piss on his shoes.

"Goddamnit!"

"I was wrong. That's funny every time."

"I ain't giving you no more beef."

I think he probably will once I put on my cute, I'm-so-innocent face. That's as close to a sure thing as Ginger used to be.

"Listen, Dave, and listen good. The Demon says you're The Chosen One. He won't let you rest until you do his bidding." I'm really selling the goods here—my tail is wagging so hard you'd guess I'd found a stash of hambones. I think smoke comes out of his ears as he mulls over my words. "He's watching you," I say. "He sees you when you're sleeping. He knows when you're awake."

"What? Is he the Santa Claus demon?" Dave laughs at that one.

"What the fuck is a 'Santa Claus?'"

"Never mind." He wipes his shoe in the dead grass and nearly falls.

"The Demon told me this morning that today is the day. He knows you have a gun, so use it already."

"You talked to him today, huh?" A smug look crosses Dave's face. "Well, then, what did he say I was doing last night?"

Dave thinks he has me, but I know from a pretty reliable source what Dave does on Tuesday nights. "He said you were watching a *Maude* rerun." I don't much get the box with the people inside—much less what a rerun may be—but that Maude bitch, her voice raises my hackles. "And he said you were jerking off to the one they call 'Carrol.'"

Since the blood rushes from Dave's face, I know my source is right. "Don't be so embarrassed, man. We all do it. Maybe not as much as you, but—"

"Shut up."

"I prefer a good blanket, all wadded up. That's an afternoon well-spent right there."

"Shut up!"

"Or a pillow. Especially if Sam's pissed me off that day, I like to leave a nice surprise for him at bedtime." And that is something worth the beating—pardon the pun.

I've hit a nerve. Sulking, Dave strides toward his house in his stained Traxx.

"Oh, c'mon, Dave. Give me a break." He reaches for the sliding-glass door. "I'm sorry, okay?"

"Screw you, Harvey." I think up a ton of jerking-off jokes when he says this, but decide I've pushed far enough. "Your whole idea is stupid," he says. "I'm not going to talk to you anymore."

"Wait!" Thoughts bombard my mind—Ginger in heat, the patty still sizzling on the grill (fuck, I love hamburger!), Ginger in heat, Cat peering at me through the pet door (I hate Cat). I need to focus; I can't let him go. And it just slips out: "The Demon, he's here."

That stops Dave. Cat steps through the door, his hind legs still inside the house. Ginger's yapping notches up to super-nag. Dave turns, and takes a couple of tentative steps back toward the fence. He squints, searching my yard as if he can see The Demon.

"Where?"

Shit, I've stepped in it now. And I'm concerned with what to tell Dave, too. With no idea what to say next, "Can't you feel him?" seems as good as anything.

"All I feel are wet feet and a sunburn coming on."

For a moment, time stops. I'm losing him. Cat's stare burrows a hole in the back of my head. I can't think clearly. I wish Cat would just leave and take his damn slitted eyes and damn nine lives. I'm suddenly afraid and I shiver.

"Oh my God, Harvey—you all right?"

I can't answer. I just quake more.

Dave runs to the fence, looking like a baby human first learning to walk. I worry he might tumble with every stride he takes. "It's The Demon, ain't it? He's possessed you."

Bingo! (Fuck, what a stupid name.) What else to do? On instinct, I flip on my back and flop about the grass. Howling adds a nice touch.

"Jesus, Harvey." Dave's voice has ratcheted an octave. His excitement adds to mine.

"Help me! The Demon, he's upon me." Benji or Lassie, they ain't got shit on me. Rin Tin Tin, eat your heart out.

The adrenaline surges as the performance continues. I spring to my feet. From the corner of my eye, my tail taunts me. I'm too excited to stop myself, and I whirl after it. Faster and faster I spin, nipping, but never quite reaching it. Then, when I'm about to quit out of exhaustion—ta-daa! I catch it. For the first time ever, I catch it.

Now what?

I shake my head, trying to yank the damn thing free, and growl in my you-just-try-to-take-that-food-from-me tone. Chomp! It may not be the smartest thing, but I'm in a frenzy, damnit. I yowl and lose hold of my tail. I come to a stop with my front paws spread wide and my head bowed. The panting comes so fast, I'm woozy.

From behind, I hear Cat enter the house. I wonder if felines can laugh, because if so, I'm sure he is. But they probably can't—their asses are wound too tight.

"Are you The Demon?" Dave asks.

"Who wants to know?" The voice is my deepest bark, and even I must admit, it's kind of intimidating.

"It is I—The Chosen One." The melodrama in Dave's delivery makes it hard for me not to break character. "What do they call you?"

My mind's a blank. "Um...Ginger. Yeah, bow to me—I am Ginger."

The barking from two blocks down reaches a frenetic pace. Here, I thought I favored the salty language, but the real Ginger is teaching me a thing or two. "Don't bring me into this," she barks. As mad at me as she sounds, I guess it doesn't matter anymore that she's fixed.

"Where's Harvey?" Dave asks. "Is he in there?"

"Tonight. You must act tonight, or I'll return tomorrow to impose my wrath." I snarl, exposing as many of the pearly whites as possible. It looks like Dave's committed an assault on his cut-offs. "Two women, am I clear?"

"Yes, Ginger." He bows his head. It looks so silly, my tail wags despite myself. He raises his head and steps backward. When he reaches the patio, he stumbles.

"And give me that hamburger." He reaches for the spatula. "Tomorrow you better have steak for Harvey. Ribeye."

Dave tosses the patty like a girl throws a ball. As I devour it—fuck, I love hamburger!—he runs inside his house. The sliding-glass door locks.

—

Cat jumps on me, waking me from my evening nap. Since this whole thing started, he's been waking me at the same time every day—right before the thing they call the news comes on the box with people inside. I don't like the news. All it does is make everybody angry.

"Nice touch yesterday with the Maude reference," Cat says. "I told you that would come in handy."

I turn my back. I can't stand looking at those eyes.

"I hope for your sake he followed through."

The music for the six o'clock news begins. Then, as if by magic, a guy with what looks like plastic hair appears in the box with people in it. I don't trust those people. I can't smell them.

"Our lead story for tonight, July 29, 1976: Two women were shot in the early morning hours in the Pelham Bay area of the Bronx." My heart jumps. No way could it be Dave. I try calming myself. It's New York for fuck's sake—there are shootings every day. "According to witnesses, a man approached the women on the street. He removed a handgun from a paper bag, fired three shots and walked away."

"He did it," Cat says. The joy in his meow is disgusting. "That worthless human showed some backbone and did it. Used the bag like I instructed and everything."

"The first victim, eighteen-year-old Donna Lauria, died at the scene. The other victim's name hasn't been released, but police say her injuries are not fatal."

"Goddamnit!" Claws rip across my back. I spin on Cat, ready to pounce. He glares at me. I cower at the malice in his eyes. Those damn eyes and damn nine lives. I've tried killing him before, but he just won't die. He's evil, I say, evil.

"He has to do better next time, Harvey"

"No. No way. I'm not doing this for you anymore."

But I look in Cat's eyes and know this is just the beginning. The summer of '76 is going to be a bloody one for New York.

JUSTAFACEINTHECROWD.COM, INC.

Now:

This is a big deal for us. Huge. Mammoth huge. As Mother would say: freakish-donkey-dangler huge. And then some.

So, I integrate. I melt into the crowd so we can perform the sabotage.

I don the old coat once again. Or should I call it a parasite? Its khaki rayon fibers leach away my individuality, suck out my spirit. It camouflages my breasts so no one can distinguish my gender. I'm an androgynous meat bag except for my shoes. Beneath the coat, I perspire in a waterfall that usually would offend my 'gentler sensibilities.' The July heat prompts a good portion of this, but it's nerves that account for the lion's share. Warm metal rubs my hip raw. The four-inch heels punish my feet. I haven't worn these dancing shoes in months, and never would have again if it wasn't such an important day. The sacrifices one makes.

But this is big. Maybe eight figures big. Eight!

Around me, the outdoor mall teems with lemmings, their chai lattes or passion-fruit smoothies in hand. Their ears glued to cell phones or fingers frivolously texting. Their need to blend in conflicting with their desire to be seen. Their obliviousness obvious.

Most wear trench coats like mine. Khaki or black or drab olive. Then, there's the fedoras keeping everybody's hairdo a mystery, not giving away a performance because passersby can't see the highlights or the extra gel to make one look just right for the cell phone cameras. It's the not-so-official uniform of the uniformed.

I'm not sure if I should be angry or feel pity. If I should crush the lemmings beneath my stiletto or attempt to educate them.

Eight figures big. Like Today Show big—like the wedding dance video with the song from that felon, Chris Brown. Like that autistic kid scoring a zillion points in his only basketball game, or that alligator thrown through the drive-thru window.

I wonder what Al Roker's really like.

Gabe. Gabe stands in position. Seeing him gives me the tingly sensation that nearly incites a case of the giggles every time. But he looks so foreign dressed like the others—like me. If I didn't know exactly where to look, I probably couldn't have picked him out at all. I steal a quick glance. That's the new norm—what's in vogue. Furtive looks. Knowing grins. Assimilating with the masses.

As I walk toward my designated mark, I bump into an elderly man with shorts hitched up to his chest. I hadn't even seen the old bastard through the sea of trench-coat clad pretenders.

"Watch it, you little..." He scrutinizes me for a moment, and his expression melts as if he's caught a heavy dose of road-kill stench. "You're going to give yourself heat stroke, you know that? You all look like a bunch of idiots."

Noticing him shakes me. He hobbles over to the Verizon bench and sits by an older woman, most likely his wife. Across the red brick street, on the AT&T bench, another elderly couple shares lunch. They wear matching jogging suits, the kind that insists so hard 'we're still pretty hip.' How could I have not seen these people before? Now that I look, it seems they occupy every bench, be it Motorola or CenturyLink or Cricket or Vonage. The first man, the one who'd chastised me, flashes a look—a look I recognize. It's the one Mother had given so often, crinkling her face in disapproval, and always at the worst possible times.

Like, in high school, on an errand to the grocery store. It's bad enough to be sixteen and out in public with your mom, but that's when Jacob Nixon and his posse crossed our path.

"Don't they realize how stupid they look?" Mother asked loudly, as Mother always did. "Didn't their parents teach them to pull up their freaking pants? It's called underwear for a reason, assholes." She emphasized 'under.'

I walked faster, hoping Mother would follow. If she stopped, only embarrassment could have resulted.

"They're just trying to be different," I said. I didn't

let on that I'd found the boys' fashion statement somewhat attractive. In hindsight, it was probably only so because of who wore the pants, and not how they actually wore them.

"Different?" she said so the boys could hear, so Jacob Nixon would hear with those perfect eighteen-year-old ears on his perfect eighteen-year-old head. "Then why are all of them doing it?"

I shake away memories of Mother. This sabotage is too important for such distraction. Gigantically important. Colossal. Eight figure big—maybe. High sevens for sure.

I check my phone for the time, suck in a deep breath of summer heat and wait.

—

Then:

It's morbid.

You're punishing yourself, but you're here anyway, crammed into the corner, back-row seat, cursing yourself for overpaying for a movie you didn't want to see. Every seat, save for the one next to you, appears full. The trench-coat clad patrons scarf down stale, eight-dollar popcorn in the half dark, waiting for the previews. Waiting for what should have been your moment.

You scan the gathering from beneath the fedora's brim. None of the others from the Happy Sunshine Crew are in attendance. When the contract fell through, you'd all agreed to boycott the event. Yet, here you sit, feet stuck to soda remnants spilled who-knows-how long ago. At least you hope it's soda.

The audience looks like a herd of Humphrey-Bogart-style, 1940's private dicks minus the personality. You see them in sepia tones. With a crowd this size, there'd have been dozens of cell phone videos posted. You mentally kick yourself again. Why'd you even come here? To torture yourself for what should have been?

See? Morbid.

Through the field of fedoras, you check again for your crew. You focus solely on what you're looking for so you don't notice if any rivals have gathered. A part of you hopes to spy somebody who'd broken their word, a target at which to level the simmering rage.

Despite the confidence in your anonymity, you slide down in the chair. As you do, he takes the empty seat.

It's the handsome man. The one who should be in commercials.

He nods. You're suddenly the girl in middle school assigned a seat in biology next to the captain of the football team. Suppress that giggle. Act cool.

You've seen him at the last two events—one for Pepsi that reached over a million hits, and a rather failing effort for the new Hyundai hybrid. Damn rain, anyway. You flatter yourself, but believe he's been watching you specifically.

He's without the get up. No fedora to mess the

thick dark hair that falls across made-for-TV face. It's a brazen display of lack of allegiance to any crew. Or maybe he's just crazy—a little dangerous.

The way his tight red t-shirt hugs his body sends a pleasant electricity through you. The cleft in his chin comes straight from central casting. He'd be the ideal addition to your crew—hell, maybe to your life. Even if it turns out he's dumb as a post, he's eye candy. He's high-def color in a black-and-white analog world. He smiles like he knows something. The giggle kicks at your tonsils, demanding its release.

The lights dim.

"I've been watching you, Denise," he says. His voice is caramel. Chocolate-coated caramel. "This is beneath you."

—

Now:

Eight figures. Ten-effin-million. Ten million voyeurs watching me. Watching me—I mean 'us'—point out their hypocrisy. Watching me (us) speak truth. And probably none of them will understand the message.

The familiar exhilaration of preparation surges, a mix of pissed-off butterflies and insistent heartburn fills me. Although now I'm a Spoiler, there's an extra charge of adrenaline. I'm in on the secret only the cool kids know.

We, the Spoilers, have hacked the Ya Ya Crew's social network, gathering intelligence for today's mission. The spot would've been for Sony or Apple or

Nintendo—some gizmo guaranteed to be the next 'have-to-have.' The Ya Ya Crew's payday is enormous.

Cameras are planted everywhere. Poorly hidden in kiosks. In the fountain. In the topiary. I chuckle quietly, thinking of the footage they'll actually catch. I don't believe it's what their campaign has in mind. Of course, most of it will never see the light of day.

But today, it's a Saturday. There's enough lemmings milling about the mall, the conduit to the tit they nurse from corporate America or corporate Japan or corporate China or corporate Wherever. Enough lemmings to guarantee plenty of video. A smorgasbord of shaky pictures coupled with muted sound. All to be unleashed on the internet, and embarrass the client— and, even better, the Ya Ya Crew.

It won't be the have-to-have. It'll be the have-to-see. Forwarded over and over and over and posted on thousands of Facebook pages by people wanting to entertain their 'friends' they've never met. Re-Tweeted a million jillion times.

Then the hits—maybe eight figures. The Today Show. Hell, maybe even Fallon. This is gargantuan.

The clock on my phone states it's nine minutes until staging time, but still no sign of the Ya Yas. The butterflies inside swell, morphing into hummingbirds. The heartburn flares so hot, a Tums the size of Pittsburgh couldn't extinguish it.

Usually, I spot a couple of crew members by now. A hint of doubt creeps into my thoughts. Why have they changed their routine at the last minute? The cameras serve as a dead giveaway that our intel is correct, that something is going down.

Usually, though, somebody has tipped their hat by this point. Eight minutes.

I allow another quick look in Gabe's direction—mostly for reassurance. A little because he's just nice to look at, though.

He's not there.

—

Then:

The patron in front of you, the one who won't take off his greasy fedora but still demands everybody else adhere to movie theater etiquette—that one—he turns to hush the handsome man and, for his efforts, receives an elbow to the nose. From the crack, you know it's broken. Your body tingles with the thrill of violence so close. It's even better than how the twenty-four-hour reality networks depict it. The handsome man—your hero, as if you needed one. Before etiquette guy can respond, handsome man lands elbow number two, knocking off the hat. More tingling. Etiquette guy slumps in his chair. His companions, seated on either side of their downed amigo, look back, give handsome man the onceover and return to their eight-dollar popcorn.

"How do you know my name?" you ask. Your words barely register as your heart tries escaping your chest.

"Don't play coy, Denise. You've seen me watching

you."

You're afraid to respond, not knowing if words or the shrieks of an adolescent girl will escape your mouth.

"I knew you'd be here." That caramel voice. He reaches over the slumped etiquette guy, grabs his eight-dollar popcorn and returns to his seat. As he slumps to your level, he says, "I think you'll enjoy this show."

The prompt serves as direction. You turn your attention to the screen and desperation you'd felt moments before returns. Your crew would have emerged for the third preview, *Kung Fu Panda Six: This Time with Chopsticks*. You steal a handful of popcorn from the handsome man and try to slow your heartbeat.

The first preview begins. "In a world where corporations no longer exist..." A collective gasp. "One man is willing to save your job..."

As the second preview nears conclusion, the handsome man squeezes your thigh. His touch barely registers as the routine you'd planned runs through your mind and you stuff more popcorn in your mouth, half-hoping you'll choke to death before the Kung Fu Panda piece rolls. You picture yourself rising from the back row, pulling out a non-existent Gatling gun, the kind from the old mobster movies, and mowing down the entire crowd just so they won't watch.

You are one morbid bitch.

"You don't have to live this life," says the handsome

man. You finally fully notice his hand on your thigh. It's over the trench coat and not sexual, but the squeeze still thrills. "I can show you a better way."

"Why?"

The handsome man sits back, dusts away stray popcorn from the cleavage of his chin and points to the screen. The second preview ends. Your heart rises to your throat, and the fight against giggling refocuses its attention so you don't cry. In your mind, you hear the 'whoa-ohs' of the beginning of *Kung Fu Fighting*, the song your flash mob crew was to dance to. It sounds so clear, it's as if it's really happening.

Then the lights go on. And it's really happening.

Dozens of moviegoers rise from their seats, shed their fedoras and trench coats, and break into choreographed moves. One two three kick, one two three punch-to-the gut. You notice your jaw agape because half-eaten eight-dollar popcorn falls into your lap, landing on your rayon trench coat. A theater full of cell phones light up, filming the flash mob.

Sandy Baggins dances in the aisle close enough you can almost spit on her. The Ya-Ya Crew's queen. Her sequined navy-blue tank catches the light perfectly as she pirouettes and then throws a weak jab. Mentally, you return the jab, crushing her jaw. Breaking her contract-stealing face, then stomping her head into an unrecognizable pulp.

No wonder the producers quit returning your phone calls. The fucking Ya Yas snaked your deal!

You turn to the handsome man. He breaks into a capped-tooth smile and points again...at the screen. "Five, four, three, two." He takes another handful of popcorn.

The screen goes white, as if God himself had struck down the silly computer-animated animals. Jack Black's voice stops mid-joke, yet the music continues. The dancing continues. Sandy Baggins' contract-stealing silicone C-cups still shimmer and bounce rhythmically beneath the sequins. But the smile has run from her face.

Behind her, a porno begins. A raunchy, filthy film that depicts acts you'd need to Google to understand their proper, as it were, names. Inhuman grunts and moans compete with the *Kung Fu Fighting* chorus. Dozens of cell phones redirect from the dancing to the screen. When the freakishly huge man on screen reaches his climax, the handsome man pulls a water pistol from his sock. He sprays Sandy Baggins in her contract-stealing face with what looks like hand lotion.

The giggle finally comes.

"Let's get out of here," he says. At that point, in that state of mind, you give into something you'd never do. But at that point, in that state of mind, you know you'd go anywhere with him.

———

In between:

His name was Gabe. He was a non-conformist, he said, and wanted me to join him. Them, rather—the

Spoilers.

I'd resisted at first. As the queen of the Happy Sunshine Crew, I'd carved quite a nice niche for myself. A modicum of fame, a few flashes of myself in internet videos, a reputation. Hell, Mother even approved in her vulgar 'way-to-fucking-go' way. I pulled quite a nice paycheck, as well, and damned sure wasn't willing to toss all of that for a man, no matter how pretty he was.

He said he'd been following me for weeks; that I noticed him earlier than he thought I would. He complimented me on my observation skills, but insisted it usually takes months for a crew member to catch onto his presence. Without the trench coat, without assimilating, he was invisible. Like all the elderly people I no longer could see, or all those who worked for a living, wore a real uniform, or anybody not in a crew. Invisible, but in plain sight.

In the end, though, I tossed it all for the handsome man. The Happy Sunshine Crew, my baby, I abandoned. For Gabe. I lived with the pangs of guilt. For what Gabe revealed to me.

Well, more so for who I thought he was. A principled man. The thrills he showed me. Perhaps it didn't hurt how many hits his insurrection received—the Spoilers. The Happy Sunshine Crew, our biggest success was the Pepsi deal. The Spoilers, even though they'd never received pay, their hit numbers dwarfed ours with almost every effort.

Their baby oil on the hardwood incident. It killed

the Gosh Golly Good Guy Crew's event for the new Nike. Some new shoe for a guy who could jump to the moon but couldn't spell it.

Or the more subtle. The Spoilers had developed a knack for infiltration, finding emails and text numbers. Changing plans. Having the Sunshine Boys do their routine where the Love for Life Crew should have been and vice-versa. (As if one didn't know, the Love for Life Crew was a hardcore group of religious pro-lifers. The Sunshine Boys? As gay as their name implies.)

Or my favorite. The Madison Square Garden Event. Yes, 'Event' is officially capitalized. The newest, greatest improvement in dishwashing soap courtesy of some mega-conglomerate chemical company. It spent almost a million dollars on their event. But the Spoilers dropped a gagillion tons of East River from the rafters during the Cuddly Puppies Crew's flash mob. The result of the mess, the combination of toxic dish soap and toxic river water, closed the 'World's Greatest Arena' for a month—for some big basketball tournament that apparently the New York team had no chance at winning anyway. But it was a big deal on all the sites.

So, as Gabe, beautiful, beautiful Gabe, courted me, I listened. I'd felt important before, hell, been damn important as the leader of one of the top flash mobs in the corporate world, but I wasn't part of a mob with him. I was one. I was me. I was...I was...

It took a solid two months before I'd participated in a Spoilers' anti event. That's what we nonconformists called everything: anti. Generic soda? Anti-Coke. Lack of media attention? Anti-propaganda. Lack of friends? Anti-establishment; nonconformist; Spoiler.

I was a Spoiler. I was a thinker. I was exciting. I was...I was...I was anti-me.

The rose-colored glasses had been ripped from my eyes. I saw truth. I saw greed. I saw no hope. Happy Sunshine my ass.

The night the epiphany occurred I'd spent in the shower. I tried washing away the corporate corruption. I tried cleansing the soul that I'd so easily sold. For hits. For attention. For confirmation that I was doing well. ('Way to fucking go.') A full bar of soap later—no corporate plug here, just generic soap, anti-soap—with my skin left red and raw, I crawled out of the shower, bawling. I crawled into the comforting arms of my handsome man. At last, I felt clean.

—

Then:

Outside the theater, you sit on a Pizza Hut bench with Gabe. Eight-dollar stale popcorn had never tasted so good.

"You'd be crucial for us," he says. "You have the insight into how crews run. I see you as an integral part of the movement."

The Movement. It sounds so silly, yet so damn exciting.

"What do you get out of all this?" you ask.

"Same as you. Didn't you feel that excitement in there?"

You answer with a smile.

"But we're sticking it to authority, like the founding fathers. With almost as much pizzazz." He pulls out his iPhone. Within seconds he finds nine videos of Jergens lotion squirting all over Sandy Baggins' contract-stealing face. "This one has almost a thousand hits already."

A thousand? It hasn't been twenty minutes. For a second, you lose yourself in the numbers.

"We need you, Denise. My goal is to take out a whole crew, one of the biggies." He tosses a popped kernel in the air and it bounces off his straight-from-central-casting chin into his mouth. "It would change the game, and we can do it with your help."

In his caramel voice, you hear 'biggies' and think Ya Ya Crew. You know you're going to do something huge.

—

Now:

Gabe. Gabe is gone.

Mannis? Him too. And James and Gabby and Adrian and Steph. Not a Spoiler in position, hell, not even in sight.

Six minutes.

What's going on? This is too Big. Yes, capital 'B' freaking Big. Where is everybody? The Spoilers? Hell, the damn Ya Yas? In this mass of trench coats and fedoras, I can't find a single soul I search for.

SLIGHTLY OFF-CENTER / 35

And I see them. Not the Ya Ya Crew. Not the
Spoilers, but the elderly couples on the benches. As I
said, somebody always tips their hat.

They're not attempting subtlety, though. Their
fingers, crooked and swollen with arthritis, point at
me. The laughter rises in unison. My panic doesn't fit
as well as my trench coat. And it hits. The AT&T bench
couple, their matching sweat suits are embroidered
with the AT&T logo. The Verizon pair wear identical
Verizon fanny packs. The Vonage bench, they each
have attaché cases, expensive ones, too, with the
Vonage logo embossed in orange. The obvious problem
had hidden in plain sight, a crew unto itself, and I, like
the lemmings, had looked past it.

My head's now on a swivel, searching. Searching
for those I belong with. Searching for the
nonconformists, the Spoilers. My so-called friends.

One minute.

The gun rubs against my hip. It's supposed to be for
protection since the corporations have turned
aggressive with their security, but as the realization of
the betrayal assails me, I'm tempted to take all these
old motherfuckers out. Tempted to show who's who,
and what's what. I catch the red light on the camera in
the topiary of a mutated turtle. Showtime. As I try to
focus on the light, movement catches my eye.

Behind the leafy turtle, by the fountain vomiting
chlorinated water mixed with the drunks' urine from
the night before, I spot the Spoilers. With an old man

in the business suit that should have been invisible, should have been seated on one of the mall's benches. With that contract-stealing whore, Sandy Baggins. I see the envelope exchanged. I see Gabe kissing said envelope with his beautiful thirty-year-old lips on his beautiful thirty-year-old face.

The old folks, the corporations themselves, they're still laughing. Despite my uniform of the uniformed, the ancient sonofabitch who I'd bumped into earlier has pointed me out. Singled me out in an assembly line of trench coats and fedoras. Like I did something special. But it would have been so damn special.

The gun, through the coat's pocket, the trigger burns against my finger. This was going to be huge. Today Show slash Fallon slash 48 Hours slash Dancing with the Lame-Ass Stars huge. The red lights, from the topiary, from the fountain, from the kiosks, they burn into me like lasers. They burn like the geriatric couples' pointing, mocking me for being the same. And it's my chance to be different.

I wonder how many hits that's worth. Would Mother say 'way to fucking go?'

Finally, I recognize some people in the crowd. Like, in the theater, where I'd looked so hard for certain people that I didn't see the Ya Yas, only now I'd been looking right past the members of the Happy Sunshine Crew. My old crew, obviously in place for a performance. I'm overcome with rage. Are they a part of this, too? Has everybody turned on me? Why else would they be here?

My goal, Gabe had said, is to take out a whole crew. One of the biggies.

The trigger, it tickles. I would be solely me, the true non-conformist because I'm the only one left. I'm alone, a buoy in a sea of obedience and submission. Way to fucking go.

And, I realize, this will be big. Huge. Mammoth huge. Freakish-donkey-dangler huge. And then some.

HATE CRIMES AND

THERAPY OVER

CREAMED CHIPPED BEEF

"Yo, Darien! It's been awhile." The waitress poured two cups of murky coffee and gave Doctor Sydney Love the once-over. Her zombie-like features displayed no acknowledgement of his injuries or the handcuffs.

She blew the thin hair from her face and turned back to Darien. "I almost didn't recognize you without your hat. You look good without that dirty old thing." She rubbed his bald pate playfully.

Darien set the .44 on the table, its business end pointed at the doctor. "You haven't seen my hat, have you Piper? Maybe somebody else wearing it?" He unpacked a Marlboro despite the red 'No Smoking' plate riveted to the booth's wall. His hand trembled, and he struggled getting the flame and cigarette to meet.

"Nah Honey, why would I?" She placed the pot on the Formica tabletop and rested a hand on her bony hip. Finally, she turned back to Sid, studying him. The doctor pleaded for help with his eyes despite the difficulty to simply look at her without cringing. "Looks like you're back in the swing of things, Darien. You roughed this one up pretty bad. What'd the piece of shit do?"

So much for help

Even through the haze of his concussion, the doctor figured Darien had finally made an error. Surely stopping at a public diner—even at such a late hour— would provide some opportunity for escape. One can't parade bloodied and bound old men around without somebody raising an eyebrow. But at hearing the waitress' comment, Sid slumped in the booth as if the emotional blow had landed with full force. Darien and he were the only patrons, so no possible conspirators existed to help him gain freedom.

Darien's lips curled into a half-smirk/half-smile as he considered the waitress' question. His bloodshot eyes focused, and confidence appeared to swell through his diminutive frame. "The old bastard likes diddling little boys. Don't you, Doc Sid?"

"Fuck you." Sid now wished he'd have pushed his patient off the wall when he had the chance.

"Fuck me? Nah—I have a driver's license. I'm too old for you." Darien blew smoke rings at the doctor's face. "Besides, you're only into them white ones, huh?"

The waitress didn't laugh. Instead she glared at Sid, disgust reflected in her hollow eyes. "You meet all types in your work, huh honey?"

"That I do," Darien said.

"Well, do me a favor: From now on, keep the perverts out of here." She left without taking their order.

Sid sat up and straightened his Italian suit jacket as much as the cuffs and pain in his shoulder allowed. His silk tie was stained beyond saving. As he noticed this, another globule of blood dropped from his head onto his lap. He forced himself to focus on the man across the table. Why'd you tell her that?"

"Why do you care?"

Sid noticed Darien studying the table and could almost see the light click on. Darien spun the gun and pointed it toward the window—facing west. Sid stifled a chuckle as the ritual unfolded.

After unfurling the silverware, Darien arranged the utensils in alphabetical order and made sure they each pointed west, as well. He proceeded onto the condiments and seasoning—ketchup, mustard, pepper, salt, and Tabasco from top to bottom. Darien then moved the Tabasco to the top, closest to Sid, perhaps classifying it as hot sauce in the alphabetical arrangement.

"I had to tell her something," Darien said. "She's not the type to just let things go—and she wouldn't have believed the truth even if I cared to share."

"Then why don't you tell me, Darien? What is the truth? Where you going with all this?"

"Don't pull any of your psychobabble bullshit on me. That's why we're in this clusterfuck in the first place." He inhaled another drag and blew the smoke hard at Sid, assaulting him with it. "Letting you talk me out of my Blackhawks hat, that was the worst thing I've ever done." He pounded the table, spilling some of Sid's coffee.

Sid spoke calmly, wanting to display he still controlled the situation. "Worse than what you did to that kid?" He paused for a reaction, but Darien only glared back. "Worse than kidnapping your psychiatrist?"

"Way I see it, if you hadn't made me get rid of my hat, I wouldn't have had to react. You brought this on yourself. All of it."

While the doctor thought it typical of a criminal to project blame onto the victim, he also thought, in this case, Darien was probably right. And Sid felt not one iota of guilt.

—

Taking on a new patient had been more of a favor than anything. Actually, rather more of an acceptance of a favor. Judge Keene's heart had been in the right place, like always, and his assessment that Sid needed to stay busy was probably correct. So the psychiatrist accepted the assignment for his friend, agreeing to evaluate the subject in his home office.

Besides, a court-ordered evaluation usually lasted only one session, five tops. Maybe it would get Sid back into the mix, drag him out of semi-retirement. Maybe he'd even find the urge to teach again—just a class or two. Although the university would never allow him back. Not after the fallout over Brian.

Sid had a lot more healing ahead before any of that'd happen, though. He'd hoped this might be a start.

So when presented with Darien White's case, Sid thought it sounded intriguing enough. Evaluating a bounty hunter—it seemed so Hollywood.

The legal file claimed Mr. White had discharged a firearm, a .44 Magnum, inside a bar. His defense had asserted a group of bikers had stolen Mr. White's hat and played keep-away while taunting him with racial slurs, and Judge Keene was inclined to rule the incident a case of self-defense. The monkey wrench proved to be Mr. White's previous run-ins with Texas' finest in law enforcement. These incidents stemmed from his unusual job and the physical force it required.

Sid's task: Evaluate Damien White and determine if there were any underlying concerns that accounted for his 'issues.'

"So, Doc Sid, do you think thirty is too young for a mid-life crisis?" That's how Mr. White had begun the first session.

In fact, the first twenty minutes consisted of him asking question after question, not allowing the doctor adequate time for response to any of them. It culminated with: "Shouldn't I be lying down for this?"

"If you'd feel more comfortable, by all means." Sid had been thrown for a moment, having almost tuned out the questions. He'd been thinking how Mr. White didn't fit Sid's mental image of a bounty hunter—too short and thin for such a rough vocation.

The bounty hunter bent and removed his alligator-skin cowboy boots. Three pennies fell to the Berber carpet that covered the basement office floor. He picked up the coins, put them back in his boots and reclined on the couch.

"Those coins signify anything to you?" Sid asked.

"Huh? Nah. See a penny, pick it up, you know. In my biz, I need all the luck I can get." Mr. White straightened the ball cap atop his head. "Kind of like my hat here. It's lucky. I don't feel right without it."

Sid had noticed the hat, worried its dust might soil the leather couch. It was ancient, and featured some sports team's logo. Probably been black at one time, it was now a faded gray, its worn brim rimmed with white sweat stains.

"So you're a Blackhawks fan?" Sid asked after he made out the logo.

"What? Oh, the hat. Nah, I hate hockey. Bunch of want-to-be athletes skating around all sissy like."

The first seeds of regret planted themselves in Sid's thoughts. Maybe he should have declined Judge Keene's offer. "Seems to me, anything would be harder on ice skates. Maybe they're even more athletic than other sports."

A laugh boomed from Mr. White. "Right. If they're so athletic, how come there's no brothers? Just a bunch of white clowns who are too small or too slow to play anything else.

"And don't get me started on all them skating fags. Hell, if chicks can do any sport as good as a guy, then that's just a gay-ass sport right there." Mr. White folded his arms. His tweed sports jacket sagged, revealing a handgun holstered to his Wranglers. "Those Olympic medals should come in pink, gayer pink, and put-it-in-my-pooper pink."

The doctor typed some notes into his laptop, his fingers punishing the keys. He took a deep breath. "You really think you need that in here?"

"What, my hat? I don't know. Suppose that depends on how good of a shrink you are." Mr. White forced another laugh, but then noticed Sid looking at the gun. "Oh, this. It's just a tool of the trade. Don't think anything of it."

"You ever shoot anybody? I mean, considering your line of work."

The bounty hunter remained silent for a long, awkward moment. "Yeah, I've shot it. Never killed anybody with it, though. You can call me a lot of things, but I'm damned sure not a murderer." He re-adjusted his hat. "Make sure you never forget that."

The previous diatribe and bringing the gun to the session were strikes one and two against Mr. White. Within the next ten minutes, he'd accumulated enough for a perfect game. He conjured a single emotion within Sid—hate. A loathing that grew exponentially with each sentence Mr. White had uttered. It wasn't simply the man's huge capacity for self-centeredness, or his hateful and prejudiced views—he'd revealed he'd only pursue white and Hispanic bond jumpers, as there were too many 'brothers' in prison already—but it was the pompous certainty in which he spoke. As if one must agree with his worldview because it was so damned obvious.

Sid had already finalized his diagnosis: G.A.D— Giant Asshole Disorder.

Checking his Rolex, the doctor wondered how he could tactfully extract himself from the session. He found himself drifting, staring at the jam-packed cherry wood bookshelves that covered every inch of office wall space. When was the last time he'd opened any of those books?

"You know, Doc Sid, I could get used to this therapy thing." Mr. White lit a cigarette without asking for permission.

Sid rubbed his temples, fighting the oncoming steam engine of a headache. "There's no smoking in the office, Mr. White."

"Call me Darien." He inhaled another long drag before extinguishing the cigarette on the coffee table. "Anyways, after *The Sopranos*, it's almost the thing for guys like me to do."

"So, you're a mobster, too?"

"I mean like tough guys and stuff. You wouldn't hypnotize me or anything like that, right?" He looked over his shoulder to view Sid. "You don't do that, do you?"

"No, Mr. White—"

"Darien."

"Hypnotherapy isn't something I practice." Sid waived away the offending smoke.

Lying back down, Darien voiced the words that sealed both he and Sid's fate. "Good. You seem okay for an old white guy and all, but I don't want to go under and you get all faggoty with me. No offense."

The hate that'd been smoldering ignited as if that one line—the timing of that one word—had been the final strike of a flint to create the perfect spark. Over the years, Sid'd heard many patients' prejudices, and they'd turned his stomach. However in this case, he'd been right—it'd been too soon.

"I think therapy would be beneficial, as well." When he spoke, it was as if the words emerged from somebody else. Yet Sid consciously knew he was forming a loose plan for the balance of the session. Nothing serious, but a little fun at Darien White's expense.

"What's that mean?"

"Well, this obsession with luck, I think it needs to be explored." Sid typed a long note into the laptop for effect. The note simply read 'fuck this fucking guy' over and over and over.

Darien sat up, his expression showing concern. "It's no obsession. Just a little—"

Sid reveled in perverse joy as the once-cocky patent squirmed. He typed faster. "Tell me, Darien, what other rituals do you perform for luck?"

"Rituals? There's no fucking rituals."

"Really? Do you avoid cracks in the sidewalk to insure you don't break your mama's back? How do you feel about black cats? Or walking under ladders?"

Darien opened his mouth, but no words formed.

Sid again checked his watch. "Sorry, that's our time."

For a moment, Darien sat with a stunned expression as he studied the psychiatrist. He slid on his boots like somebody dressing after a sexual experience they knew they'd later regret.

Sid thought he and Brian's memory were somewhat vindicated. He held no intention of seeing Darien White ever again.

—

Darien sipped his coffee, welcoming the burn in his throat because it confirmed he could still feel. Thoughts bombarded him, but none stuck. No idea materialized on how to handle the doctor, and his memory was fuzzy on why they were even at the diner.

He glared at the table. Doc Sid's expensive haircut was nothing but a memory as gray hair swirled about his head in disarray. Blood had congealed in the tufts, creating dark clumps. The gash across his forehead still seeped fluid.

What if Darien hadn't gone back that next day? He didn't need to—his lawyer had said the evaluation was already complete. However, the more Darien had thought about the first session, the more questions he had, and he hadn't even broached what he truly wanted to discuss.

He almost hadn't gone through with it. Even as he'd been walking up the path to the doctor's house, he'd considered turning back. Then he noticed how he timed his steps, how he'd managed to miss the cracks in the concrete.

The waitress woke Darien from his trance when she slid the plate in front of him.

"Shit on a shingle with two eggs, basted—your usual." She also slammed a plate of dry toast in front of the shrink. "You want me to get him anything else?"

"Nah. Fuck him."

The waitress picked up the plate and spat on the toast. "No charge for the special sauce."

Across the table, Doc Sid undid his napkin and used it to wipe his face. Blood ringed the cuffs. A hint of guilt crept into Darien's disassociated thoughts, but he quickly pushed it aside when he saw the doctor's silverware randomly spread across the table.

"Anything else then?" the waitress asked."

"Huh?" Darien continued looking at the knife spoon and two forks. His heartbeat accelerated, and he puffed on the cigarette. "Actually, I have a question."

"Yes, Honey, a blowjob will still cost you fifty bucks."

The thought of her almost lifeless face bobbing on him gave him chills, but he played along with their long-standing joke and forced a smile. "This is more of a philosophical one, Piper. You think you can murder someone if you're already dead?" He eyed the shrink, waiting for a reaction that never came.

The waitress shook her head. "I haven't given that much thought, and I'm not about to start now. I'll get you some more coffee." She walked away, but turned to shoot Darien a curious look before disappearing into the kitchen.

Doc Sid bounced one of the forks in a drumbeat by pushing on the tines and releasing. Darien wondered if the shrink was taunting him. The urge to take the utensils and make sure they all faced west—toward progress because that's where the sun heads—ate at Darien. Then he realized that was the doctor's silverware, and the bad things would happen to the shrink. Anything bad that happened to Doc Sid was a good thing for Darien.

"You're still thinking of hurting yourself," Doc Sid said. "Can't say I blame you with the situation you've put yourself in." He bounced the fork faster. "Are you going to kill me, Darien?"

While the thought of squeezing one off right between the doctor's baby blues was pleasing on some level, Darien wouldn't cave now. "You know I'm not a murderer."

"Yes. We've been through that tonight."

As Darien cut his eggs, he tried blocking out Doc Sid's voice. With the channels in his mind flipping like a possessed television, he didn't need the old fucker to manipulate him anymore. If he could just find his hat, everything would be okay—no more rituals, no more unsettling thoughts. Surely, as much as the doctor had fucked with him over the last few months, the sick bastard had to have lied about the fate of the hat. He had to.

"You know, Darien, it's not too late. You can get out of this without anybody else getting hurt."

Wouldn't it be wonderful if that were true? "Toast not good enough for you, Doc? After all the extra work Piper put in it and all?"

The shrink flashed him that smile—the condescending one that said he knew something more than Darien. Doc Sid picked up the toast with both hands, the handcuffs stretching to their limit, and took a bite. Darien washed down his mouthful of egg with coffee and waited to see if he'd be able to keep it inside.

"This Piper, she a girlfriend of yours? Quite the looker that one," Doc Sid said.

"Shut the fuck up."

"Is she sick?"

"I don't know. Probably should have asked that before you ate her loogie sandwich."

"Something wrong with her?"

Darien knew the questions were leading somewhere. Just like the shrink eating the toast—it was all connected, all methods to manipulate Darien. "There's something wrong with all of us, isn't there,

Doc?"

"I guess there is." He sipped his coffee and pushed away the remaining toast. "Especially with you."

—

Darien couldn't stop his finger from shaking as he'd held it inches from Doc Sid's doorbell. He hadn't slept in two days, anticipating the impending session. "Shit!" He stomped out his cigarette and began swiping at his forearms, alternating between them while he counted to a hundred as fast as possible. When he'd finished counting, he was swiping his left arm—bad. He started the ritual again.

After a couple of more tries, he finally ended on a century while on his right arm—good. He was ready to re-try the doorbell, but again stopped inches short. Sweat poured off as the noonday sun roasted him. Something wasn't right. He adjusted his Blackhawks hat and started swiping and counting.

He chided himself. Ending on the right was good enough—should have been good enough—but he was now procrastinating. For four and a half months he'd been trying to tell Doc Sid why he really always returned for the sessions. Today he was going to spit it out.

But he didn't stop swiping.

Why was he so afraid? Before the question completely formed, he knew the answer. Doc Sid had done so much and at no charge because Darien had no health insurance. The sessions were free, and the doctor not only paid for the prescriptions, he had them waiting at the office. After all that, Darien wanted to keep his past from the shrink; didn't want the doctor to know Darien was a bad guy.

Part of him wanted to flee from the doorstep and escape down the path lined with manicured dogwoods. It was too late, however, as Doc Sid opened the door.

"Darien?" He stood in a white monogrammed bathrobe with a martini in his hand. A glassy haze covered his eyes, and he hadn't yet shaved. "Were we to meet today?"

"Forgot again, huh?"

The doctor hesitated, staring blankly. "No. Of course not. Still wearing that damn hat? None of the new routines working?"

Darien slipped past the doctor and headed for the basement. Butterflies swirled in his belly when he entered the office. "Cleaning lady have the week off?"

"Something like that. Doc Sid downed the rest of the martini and plopped into a leather recliner. "The new meds helping at all? You look like hell."

"Really? You should talk. That robe makes you look like a fag." Darien slid off his boots and turned them over to prove he still wasn't carrying the pennies. A small victory that he could point to as progress.

The shrink didn't seem to notice, though. He rubbed his temples with one hand, and the muscles in his jaw clenched. "What about the meds, Darien? Do you need some more?"

"I'm low on the blue ones." He couldn't remember any of the pills' actual names—not after the first week anyway. And since the doctor gave them to him in baggies, there was no label to read. All he knew was Doc Sid had emphasized to take them regularly or Darien could end up really screwed in the head. "The new ones make me jittery, though. Can't sleep."

The doctor raised his head and smiled. "That's to be expected. Give them a couple of weeks." He grabbed his laptop and flipped it open. "Shall we begin?"

This was it. Time stopped as Darien waited for his voice to engage—waited to confess. The silence was thick.

In his mind, he was there again, as if he could reach out and pull back the kid. He smelled the subway exhaust and dried urine; saw the grimy white and green tiles decorating the platform walls; experienced the eerie solitude of a Tuesday at two a.m. beneath the streets of Manhattan.

He'd been an NYC cop for less than a month and was working on a joint operation with the Transit Authority to crack down on subway system muggings. For the most part, it'd been pretty uneventful, but he was finally a cop. He'd survived the academy and the nonstop needling about his lack of size and fulfilled his promise. Pop would have approved. Everything in life was coming together.

Until he saw Eldrich Irons standing alone on the platform. The fifteen-year-old was one of the suspects linked to the latest rash of muggings, and Darien had seen his picture a thousand times in the last month. The kid belonged to a group not organized enough to be a gang, but reportedly armed enough that they could have been.

Darien's heart thundered and he put out his cigarette with his foot. The suspect hadn't noticed him, instead he leaned out over the platform and looked for the next subway. His hands remained in a satin Yankees jacket and he fidgeted as if he needed a bathroom. He wore a black baseball cap, the bill turned backwards. Darien ducked behind a column. He'd wait until the train approached so Eldrich Irons would be less likely to hear footsteps.

A slight rumbling filled the space but grew louder quickly. Darien quivered with a nervous excitement and anticipation he hadn't felt since before his first track meet in high school. He slid from behind the graffiti-covered column and unholstered his firearm. The thumping in his chest grew so violent, it throbbed through his arms.

As the volume rose, Darien broke, his adrenaline pumping to the point he could almost fly. A set of headphones plugged the suspect's ears. The train's light illuminated the dark tunnel. Darien's pace seemed to match the subway's. As he reached for the suspect's shoulder, the kid turned. His eyes opened comically wide, and he stepped back.

Darien missed with the first grab. As the kid fell, he

reached again, but only pulled back the ball cap. A slight scream rose before the crushing of bones and the subway's brakes.

The doors opened in unison with a loud hiss, but nobody exited the train. Did the driver not see the fall?

Darien stood with hat in hand, waiting for somebody to wake him. After a short eternity, the subway pulled away. Darien peered over the platform edge, the tracks too dark to see anything. He pulled free his flashlight. His hands shook so hard, he needed both to turn it on. When he lowered the light, he closed his eyes. He listened for any signs of life, but only heard the train in the distance. Swallowing hard, he opened his eyes and saw nothing. The body was gone. A pool of blood had formed between the tracks, and it streaked toward the departed subway.

His body went limp, as if it were he who the train had struck. He looked to his hand like the hat could bring the kid back. Through the forming tears, he saw the Chicago Blackhawks emblem.

"Darien, are you with me?" Doc Sid asked.

"What?"

"You haven't said anything. It's not like you to be the quiet type."

Darien nodded. He half-tried to smile.

"Wait a second," the doctor said. "Isn't today Tuesday?"

"No, it's Thursday."

"Darien, I might be getting up there, but I'm not

senile yet. Your appointment may be Thursday, but today is most definitely Tuesday."

"Really?" Darien tried recreating a timetable in his mind. When was the last time he'd been to the doctor's? Hell—what did he have for breakfast today? "Are you sure? I can't be losing it that bad, can I?"

The doctor grinned and pointed to the Rolls Royce calendar pinned to the door. "Since you're here, we might as well have your session anyway. Sound good to you?"

"Sure." But Darien didn't really comprehend what he'd said. He was still trying to piece together days in his head. Even looking at the calendar, it appeared that the day was Tuesday. Yet, the shrink seemed so sure, Darien accepted he was wrong, but couldn't figure out how.

"That's fantastic, because I want to address your lucky hat today. I think it's time you rid yourself of it permanently."

—

Sid glared as Darien chewed the creamed chipped beef. The bounty hunter's eyes focused on nothing and Sid questioned how much of the original Darien still resided in that bigoted soul. Then again, he wondered if any of his true self still existed, either.

While Sid hadn't intended on turning Darien White into an experiment, the asshole kept returning. Every time he rang the doorbell, all Sid could see staring back at him were the bullies that'd killed Brian.

Darien removed a piece of gristle and placed it on the plate. "So, what you think, Doc?"

"I think I'm tired and hungry and I want to go home."

"Oh wah. What about my question? You think a dead person can commit murder?"

Sid wondered if what was left of the potato salad of Darien's mind could in any way be forming a plot. "You think you're going to come back from the grave for me, Darien?"

"I may be a 'mess,' isn't that how you put it? An 'OCD, suicidal paranoid mess?'" He inhaled off the cigarette before tossing it to the floor and rubbing it out. "But I'm not messed up enough to be believing in any ghosts."

The bounty hunter shoved another forkful into his mouth. Although the entrée looked like wallpaper paste peppered with slime-covered flies, it still smelled great. Sid hadn't eaten for hours.

"You know what I keep coming back to, Doc? Why'd you do this? Why me? I never did you wrong in any way."

Sid thought Brian hadn't done anything wrong to deserve his fate, either. That it was people exactly like Darien White, ignorant, hateful assholes, who'd killed the only reason Sid had for caring about anything.

Brian had changed Sid's life the moment he'd walked through the office door. A confident smile had graced the young man's face, unlike most of the other freshmen who appeared rattled at their first meeting with an advisor. Brian extended his hand, looked Sid in the eyes, and shook with a grip that could have forged iron.

"Brian Henke," he said. "Freshman extraordinaire."

Part of Sid wanted to play the curmudgeon and say 'we'll see about that,' but the student's energy was too great. He was blond and chiseled with a Kirk Douglas dimple in his chin—although too young to know who Kirk Douglas was. He looked the part of everybody's All-American. All he needed was the letter sweater, preferably in baby blue to highlight his eyes. Instead, he wore a tight-fitted white t-shirt with a Pi Kappa Alpha pin.

"You're rushing the Pikes, Mr. Henke?"

"Who the hell's this Mr. Henke? I won't respond unless you call me Brian, agreed?

Sid couldn't help but laugh, probably harder than the quip had warranted. "Well, Brian, I hope you don't mind me saying so, but I think the Pikes are an immature conglomeration of fart noises and a waste of oxygen. No offense."

Brian lifted his forearm to his head, feigning he'd been wounded. "Kind sir, how dare you speak of my brothers in such a derogatory tone? You have besmirched my honor." He then leaned forward in a conspiratorial manner, teeth glowing as he smiled even wider. "Truth be told, I agree. But Dad was a Pike, so it's kind of pre-ordained."

The rest of the meeting was more of a comedy act, and somehow by the end, Sid had advised Brian to take several classes Sid himself would be teaching the next semester.

He'd thought Brian would merely serve as eye candy, a diversion from the monotonous regurgitation of abnormal psych theories and the history of Jung. However, early in the spring semester that freshman year, the office visits began. A short question here evolved into a larger discussion of the DSM-IV which turned into a lunch over the bullshit of Freud and then finally, after debating the merits of various depressant therapies, the sex. It'd happened about that fast.

Their relationship—kept tightly secret for the sake of Sid's job and Brian's status in the frat house—lasted over two years. Early on, Sid had thought Brian must have been using him for favorable grades, but as time passed, the doctor grew more comfortable. He allowed himself to fall in love and be happy. For two years, they both were.

Around the middle of Brian's junior year, things began changing, though. Brian withdrew, a drastic change from his gregarious usual self. He also quit the hockey team suddenly.

Sid didn't press, waiting instead for Brian to initiate any conversation about possible problems. Sid worried Brian was ready to leave. Maybe if Sid weren't so insecure about their age difference, he would have pressed the issue. Maybe things would have turned out different.

On a late February morning, Brain asked if he could move in with Sid, away from the frat house. As thrilled as Sid should have been—he'd been proposing such an arrangement for over a year—a feeling of trepidation coursed through him.

Later that same day, Sid opened the college newspaper while eating lunch. An odd, ominous personal ad had been placed:

"Brother Pikes—beware your shower time! BH is watching."

From there, things deteriorated quickly. The next Tuesday, Brian barged into Sid's office. Tears ran down his cheek unapologetically.

"I need a key to the house." Phlegm clogged his voice.

Sid stood and walked around his desk to comfort his boyfriend. "What's happened? What's wrong?"

"Just give me the fucking key, okay?"

Sid hesitated. He wanted to envelop Brian in his arms, to absorb all the emotion. Instead, he reached into his pocket, slid the key off the ring and gave it to Brian. Brian left without thanking him.

Allowing Brian a small head start, Sid left the office. Brian had already disappeared from the hall, so Sid ran from the psychology building in search of him.

Outside, a buzz permeated the commons. Giggles and guffaws filled the air, and a line had formed outside the student center. Sid's blood pressure rose, and all moisture abandoned his mouth.

He cut in line and entered the building. Raucous laughter echoed through the halls. Sid recognized its tone—not the jovial, good-time expression of joy, rather the mocking timbre when the laughs come at some unfortunate soul's expense. Sid's heart beat so hard it felt uncomfortable. In the confusion, he couldn't immediately identify the 'joke.'

Dozens of notebook-sized papers lined the hall. They alternated between a single letter on one piece followed by a black-and-white photocopied picture on the next. The pictures showed a controversial print from the university art gallery years earlier. In it, Bert and Ernie of Sesame Street were posed with Ernie bent and Burt pumping him from behind. Except Ernie's face had been replaced with a picture of Brian. Each picture contained a different dialogue bubble from Brian. 'I likey the dick;' 'I'm such a fag;' 'Daddy would be so proud.'

Nausea overwhelmed Sid. His extremities numbed and his head spun. He couldn't fathom the pain Brian must be experiencing, but Sid hurt enough for the both of them. Only as an afterthought, did he put together the letters. 'Brian Henke is a faggot.'

The message led down the length of the hall into the atrium where the scope of the nightmare morphed into an epic horror. A billboard-sized blowup of the picture hung from the ceiling. The dialogue bubble read: 'Will suck cock for food—especially sausage.'

Sid pin-balled through the crowd, their laughter suffocating him. He couldn't escape the center fast enough, and the claustrophobia resulted in sweat dripping off him. He pushed students out of his way as the door seemed set further away than he remembered. Once in the fresh air, Sid fell to his knees, buried his head in his hands and bawled.

The drive home took forever. Brian wouldn't answer the phone and ignored Sid's texts. Sid pulled in the driveway and exited the Mercedes without killing the engine. He sprinted to the front door, stumbling up the path. But once he reached the porch, something stopped him. He knew.

None of Brian's fraternity brothers or hockey teammates bothered with the funeral.

And now, an ass like Darien White had the audacity to complain that he'd been wronged. Shaking his head, Sid laughed. "Why'd I do it? That's easy. I did it because you let me. You simply kept returning for more."

Darien slammed the fork into the table. "I would've never kept coming back if you hadn't fucked me up so bad." He hurled the fork, missing Sid's head by inches. By the sound, if it had connected, it would have caused serious damage. "I came to you for help!"

"You came to me because you're a smug little fuck who couldn't take anybody saying you might have a fault." Spittle flew as Sid yelled. "You had to prove to me that you were all the smug shit you thought you were."

The doors from the kitchen banged open. The waitress strode to the table, anger etched in her hideous features. "That's enough for today, Darien. You and your pervert friend get the fuck out of here." She tossed the check on the table. "And you damn sure better tip me enough to deal with all your shit."

———

The call had awoken Sid in the middle of the night—never a good sign. When he'd heard Darien's voice on the other end, it made matters all the worse.

"I need to see you." Darien said. His voice was monotone, matter-of-fact.

Sid was surprised to hear from the bounty hunter. Darien had skipped their appointment after Sid hadn't provided more amphetamines. There'd been no contact for two weeks, and Sid had begun checking the obituaries—usually with a smile across his face. "What time is it?"

"Early. Or late. I don't know."

"What's going on, Darien?"

"I'm on a roof. I think I've really lost it."

Finally, Sid thought.

He now followed the navigation system's directions, still half-drunk which was how he often woke lately. He'd passed out in his suit and tie. So, after combing his hair and rinsing his mouth with another martini, he entered the car ready for anything. The Mercedes turned down empty street after empty street, every stoplight flashing yellow. The sense of solitude was stifling.

Then, Sid turned on the avenue containing the address Darien had directed him to. There, a chorus of flashing lights danced off the glass and brick buildings. Two squad cars, a fire engine and an ambulance blocked the way. Sid parked on the street, away from the confusion, but he'd need to circumvent the action to enter Darien's apartment building. He concentrated on walking straight, especially with so many police around.

"Is he going to die?" a woman asked one of the policemen. Panic sounded in her voice.

A small surge of adrenaline ran through Sid. He wondered if Darien had completed the deed.

"Paramedics said he's got a pretty nasty concussion and a few broken bones—nothing life threatening, though. Probably take a few days in the hospital," the cop said. "You said you never seen the other guy? All this was over a baseball hat?"

The realization of what Darien had done brought on a slew of emotion. Horror for the victim was balanced by a satisfaction as to how far Darien had degenerated. The excitement of seeing the degeneration first-hand was offset by the fear of the loss of it all. In some strange manner, his punishment of Darien, the experiment, had been a vessel for Sid's mourning. If everything ended tonight, how would he continue to preserve Brian's memory?

The doctor slipped into the apartment building and

entered the elevator. He pressed the button for the top floor, the tenth. As he rode up in the dimly lit elevator, he wondered what state he'd find Darien in. The exit lay at the end of the hall. Sid traversed the garish carpet held together in several areas with duct tape.

He followed the two flights of stairs to the roof. His footsteps echoed off the metal and cinderblocks. Sid hesitated before opening the door. Whatever lay on the other side would change him forever.

Inhaling a deep breath, he pushed the cold metal bar and walked into the night. The effect of alcohol combined with the roof's unfamiliar surroundings, disoriented him. He couldn't see Darien at first, but as he gained his bearings he knew exactly where to look.

He turned to the west—of course—and there was the bounty hunter, sitting on the building's edge with his legs dangling. He bent his head toward his chest, and his shoulders slouched like those of a beaten man. For a moment, Sid felt a small pang of regret.

Then he remembered the thousands of occurrences where Darien had said 'faggot' and the nonchalant incidents of homophobia he'd leisurely peppered into conversation. And while there were other people to blame for Brian's death, there weren't any more convenient villains.

Sid thought how all of Darien's attitudes had led to Brian's demise. A vision of Brian fucking a Muppet filled Sid's mind, and it was all he could do to not burst into a sprint and shove Darien from his perch.

"Thanks for coming, Doc." Darien spoke without turning around.

Sid approached slowly, the roof crunching beneath his Kenneth Coles.

"He'll be all right, won't he?" Darien turned back and exhaled a large puff of smoke. The flashing lights below reflected off his tears. "I saw you walk past them. Did they say anything?"

Sid reached for the short brick wall on which Darien sat. His knees wobbled and he dare not look at the action below. "You're not afraid they'll look for you here?"

"Shit, Doc. I find people for a living. Hiding in plain sight is always the best policy."

"So, what happened?"

"He had on a Blackhawks hat. For a second, I thought it was mine." Darien wiped his nose with the sleeve of his jacket. I just lost it. I didn't know what I was doing."

"They said he'll make it." Sid didn't know why he reassured Darien.

"Good." Darien flicked the short cigarette into the sky and blew out a final breath of smoke. "I'm no murderer."

Below, a siren screamed to life. Sid assumed the ambulance was leaving. "Not a murderer. I've always wondered about your phrasing there. It seems odd. You've never said you're not a 'killer,' or you've never 'killed' someone. There's a distinction in your mind, isn't there?"

Darien nodded, but didn't appear to measure his words. He spoke like he'd practiced the answer a million times. "Murderers do it on purpose." Darien took out another cigarette, but the breeze negated his attempts to light it.

"You know, Doc, you were wrong." He flicked the Bic again to no avail. "I did need that hat. I really needed it. Since I gave it up, everything's gone wrong. Things sucked a little after I got rid of the pennies, but shit really hit the fan once I let you take my hat."

Sid looked for the bulge beneath Darien's jacket. Sure enough, the ever-present gun hung on the bounty hunter's hip. For five months now, Sid had been careful not to push too hard; careful to at least appear concerned for Darien. After Sid had begun the experiment, Darien was no longer stable, and the gun always played as a wild card. Tonight, however, was the time to push. Maybe Sid's buzz resulted in poor judgment, but Darien was in the perfect state. Sid could end this now.

"Why'd you call me tonight, Darien?"

The bounty hunter looked like he believed the answer was obvious. "I guess I didn't have anybody else. You've tried so hard to help me—I'm sorry. Guess I haven't been your most successful patient, huh?"

Sid rested against the wall, facing away from the street. "I'd say you're my most successful, but you shouldn't have called me. If you have nobody else, then

I'm afraid you have nobody at all."

Darien's expression crumbled into confusion.

"I hate you Darien White. I hate everything you stand for; I hate the air you breathe. The only reason I kept seeing you was to see how bad I could fuck you up.

"The pills, the 'therapy,'" Sid made air quotes as he spoke. "All of it was to see if I could turn you into a mess. And I succeeded. You're an OCD, suicidal, paranoid mess."

The bounty hunter sat in stunned silence. Sid watched Darien process the information while keeping an eye on the bulge in the jacket.

"You gave me pills to turn me crazy?"

"Oh, did I give you pills. I gave you Prozac and lithium and amphetamines and OxyContin and testosterone. Hell, I even made sure you wouldn't get pregnant."

Darien glared in disbelief. "What the fuck are you talking about?"

"You, Darien, have been on the pill for two months. Did you miss your period?"

"Are you fucking serious?" Darien began swiping at his arms.

"As a heart attack. I've pumped you so full of mind-altering drugs, of behavioral drugs, of hormones, I'm actually impressed it took you this long to crack.

"You know all them rituals we devised? The ones so you could get past your good-luck charms? I think I turned you OCD—I didn't know that was even possible."

Darien continued swiping. His breathing hastened.

"Of course, you're so far gone now, they'll probably have to institutionalize you. That is if they don't send you away for what you did to that kid down there. I'm sure all the people you caught jumping bail would really enjoy a prison reunion."

Darien stood, but continued swiping. Sid's heart thundered, as he thought this might be the moment.

"One hundred," Darien said. He was on his right arm, but Sid couldn't recall what that meant. "My hat. I want you to bring me my fucking hat."

Sid guffawed. "I think there's a few more things you need to worry about before your stupid hat."

The kick came from nowhere. It landed squarely across the bridge of Sid's nose and knocked him to the roof. Sid was immobilized equally by the pain and the shock. It felt like an explosion of shrapnel inside his head.

Darien pounced. He grabbed Sid by the throat. "I want my fucking hat!" He kneed Sid in the ribs—another explosion in the chest. "Where's my hat, old man?"

Sid tried forcing a smile, at least appearing defiant despite the overwhelming fear. " I burned it." The words emerged in gasps. "I torched it the very day you gave it to me, and I pissed out the fire."

Another knee to the ribs. "NO!" Handcuffs bound Sid's wrists before he realized Darien even had any.

Darien stood and yanked Sid up by the arm. A burning erupted in Sid's shoulder, and he worried it'd been dislocated. By the time he found his balance, Darien had the Magnum pulled.

"What are you doing to do with that, Darien? Murder me?" Sid talked pure bluster, as he feared that was exactly the plan.

"Fuck you. Start walking."

Sid followed the instruction, heading toward the exit. Darien opened the door and gestured with the gun for Sid to go first.

"Where you taking me?"

"I don't know." Darien kicked the doctor in the back, knocking him down the stairs. Sid counted the bruises as they accumulated. "But I'm kind of hungry."

—

Darien shoved the shrink through the Yellow Rose Dinner and Fill station parking lot, toward the 1994 Chevy Impala. The old man's feet kicked up a dust storm as he stumbled.

"Hasn't this gone on long enough?" A hint of anxiety tainted Doc Sid's voice. "Think about it, Darien. Either you're going to let me go, or you're going to murder me."

Darien placed his boot on the doctor's ass and shoved. "For somebody who'd thought up such an elaborate plan to fuck me up, you sure don't have much of an imagination."

Doc Sid turned to look at Darien. The old man's

face displayed a hint of fear. Darien shoved again, and the shrink landed against the Impala with a loud thud. Darien opened the passenger-side door and unlocked the back. After pulling open the back door, he gestured for Doc Sid to enter.

"No." The shrink puffed his chest in defiance. "I won't get in that car. You'll have to murder me first." He emphasized the word, 'murder.'

Darien undid the gun's safety. Doc Sid's eyes widened in surprise. The bounty hunter fired a warning shot well over the old man's head.

"I can shoot you in a whole bunch of places that won't kill you. We both know you're getting in that car. It just depends on what shape you want to ride in, and I'd appreciate it if you didn't bleed anymore on my seat."

Shaking visibly, the doctor relented. After he slid into the car, Darien wove the shoulder belt through the shrink's hands and latched into the opposite seat's outlet. He then used the modified waist belt, the one specifically altered for helping him restrain the bail jumpers he transported, and latched into the outlet closest to the doctor.

"Darien, please—" Fear engraved itself further into Doc Sid's expression.

I've had enough of your lip. Sit back, shut up, and enjoy the fucking ride." Darien walked to the driver's side. As he opened the door, a flash on the gravel parking lot caught his eye. Darien stooped for the penny. He held it up to the yellow parking lot lights and smiled. Before sliding it into his boot, he kissed it.

A calmness swelled through him as he started the car. Despite his horror of the shrink's betrayal, it seemed right that Darien had resumed control. The Impala choked and sputtered, then growled to life. Darien realized he knew how this would all play out long before they'd entered the diner.

He pulled onto the deserted tow-lane highway, clicked on his high beams, and waited for opportunity. In the rear-view mirror, he spotted Doc Sid chewing on his bottom lip. "What you thinking back there, Doc?"

The shrink met Darien's eyes. "Contemplating your question. I think maybe a dead man can commit murder, don't you?"

Darien laughed—an old-fashioned belly laugh that he hadn't enjoyed since Doc Sid had started him on the pills. "Nah. You're splitting hairs there. If you're dead, you can't act. If you can't act, it just follows—you can't murder."

Apparently, that wasn't the response the doctor had hoped for. He thrashed around violently against the seatbelts. "Goddamnit! Let me go."

Darien pushed Impala's lighter, then lit a cigarette. The green LED speedometer reported his speed as sixty-five.

"I don't know what you planned, Darien, but you'll regret it."

The headlights of an oncoming vehicle appeared in

the opposite lane. Darien floored it.

"Jesus Christ! What are you doing?" Sid's face morphed into an assembly of dread.

The speedometer reached seventy-five. Darien grinned widely in the rear-view mirror before cutting the headlights.

"You're going to kill us!" The horror ratcheted the shrink's voice an octave higher. "You'll be a murderer."

Darien calmly inhaled off the cigarette. As the oncoming lights neared, it became clear they belonged to a semi truck. The Impala's engine roared louder, drowning out some of Doc Sid's screams. The display read one-hundred-two.

"Don't do this, Darien," the shrink yelled. "You don't want to die a murderer. You said that a hundred times."

Darien picked up the gun from the passenger seat. "I won't. He secured the barrel in his mouth. The truck was less than thirty yards away, and Darien swerved into its lane. The speedometer claimed the Impala traveled at one-hundred-eleven miles per hour. Before Darien pulled the trigger, he realized they were headed west—toward progress.

ON YOU; IN YOU

"They crawl on you," Patient 3442 said. His voice sounded hollow and distant trough the speaker. "Tiny, dirty little things that multiply in your hair, in your armpit, in your crotch. It's not the crawling that makes you itch, though. A little, sure, but it's more the biting. Now that'll make you scratch 'til you bleed.

"You picture them burrowing in you, laying their eggs. Thousands of those fucking eggs—incubating, hatching. Always hatching, with more of those malevolent sons-a-bitches that start crawling on you immediately. You envision mandibles ripping away your skin. You can almost hear them suck your blood."

The patient scratched himself, running his fingernails over the welts covering his upper arms. His skin varied from bruised to scabbed to scarred. Running his hand over his shaved head, he flicked away the collected ooze from his fingers. He rose from the stool, walking to the glass partition. Footsteps stomping across the metal floor resonated through the speaker.

"The worst part, though, is when you sleep. They fill your dreams—images of them grinding over each other like some sort of parasitic orgy. You dream of this and see it happening on your own scalp. And you wake, itching—not just from those little robotic fuckers, but from the crawling sensation the dream left on you. It feels so...dirty."

The doctor stopped tapping data into his digital notebook. He leaned forward, pressing the intercom button. "Did you say something about robots?"

"Don't even, Doc. Don't fuck with me. I know you're in on it, and you know what I know. Let's not waste our time."

The doctor nodded slightly. Extending his arm, he adjusted his D-con suit and resumed tapping notes.

"Like I said," the patient continued, "you always feel dirty. You get out of the shower, start scratching and jump right back in. You can't escape thoughts that you're one big steak to thousands of them little bastards. But that's just the first phase. You don't really know what they are yet, but how could you really? It's all too fantastic to believe, isn't it?"

The doctor scooted closer to the glass, better examining the various rashes and scars. The patient wore a white pair of briefs—tighty whities—but the pus seeping from the gashes underneath had stained them into some undeterminable hue. The wounds covering his chest were particularly bad. The doctor couldn't discern if they were from an infection or burns from the many chemical bath treatments.

"It happens so fast," the patient said. "One day you're just sickened, thinking you, of all people, are infested with lice. But within a week, they've taken over your life. By the end of the next week, they've got your mind.

"When they first burrowed through my skull, that was the most painful part. It began on the monorail. I was going to pick my son up for the weekend. Never made it though."

The patient picked at a scab on his forearm. Rolling the part he removed between his thumb and middle finger, he flicked it at the glass.

"I remember how tight I clutched the newspaper pages, trying to keep myself from scratching in public. The pain began as an unpleasant tingling. I had to let go of the paper, sneaking in a scratch, but that just seemed to piss them off. They started boring then, tiny jackhammers pounding into my scalp."

The patient paced about the tiny cell. He held his hands to his head, pressing on his temples while he closed his eyes. The doctor noted tears streaming down the patient's face.

"I feel all the little holes. My skull must look like some moldy sponge, tiny caves lined with more of them fucking eggs."

The patient dropped his hands from his head, scratching his torso in violent, fitful motions. He screamed and began sobbing.

"Can I get you some water?" the doctor asked. "Would you like a break?"

"I don't have time for a break, Doc. You know they got me bad."

Again, the doctor nodded. Inside the suit, sweat

SLIGHTLY OFF-CENTER / 77

tickled his neck. He kept entering the testimony into the tablet.

"And I know they're going to get you, too, Doc."

The doctor quit tapping with the stylus. He looked up, finding the patient glaring at him. The man stood mere inches from the partition, his breath fogging the glass. Lips bent into a defiant snarl, he wiped away the remaining tears from his face.

The patient smiled. The whiteness of his teeth glowed against the discolored look of his skin. "But you probably know that, don't you?"

Pretending to focus on the notebook's small screen, the doctor said, "Please continue. You were on the monorail?"

Patient 3442 released a small, taunting laugh. "Yeah, the monorail. That's where I lost it." He returned to the stool and sat. Running fingers over his thighs, he dug the nails into flesh. "There are some damn attractive women in that monorail car, too. Embarrassed the shit out of me. I screamed in agony, unable to control myself. Scratching my head as hard as I could, I ended up falling. With the security on those trains what it is, the marshal was all over me. He Tasered my ass.

"During the paralysis from the shock was the first time I heard them. That tiny hum started in the back of my head, like an annoying electric razor. For a good thirty seconds, all I heard was them grinding through the bone.

"Wait until you hear that, Doc. You won't know what's worse, the pain or that tinny, buzzing drone."

The doctor jabbed the intercom button. "That's quite enough, sir! You can stop that scratching as well. The treatments have killed any remaining lice. I assure you, we're both quite safe."

"I can see that," the patient replied. "Nice suit there, Doc. Hazmat orange looks good on you."

"It's regulation. Now, may we continue?"

"Fuck you."

The doctor squeezed the notebook tight. He clenched his jaw, inhaling deeply.

"You really think I'm clean? You're deluding yourself, Doc." Patient 3442 rose again from the stool, stomping over to the glass. The echoes thundered through the speaker. "Bring your glass over here."

"What?"

"That big fucking magnifying glass you were using to look at my back. Roll it over here."

"Sir, am I going to have to enable the floor?"

"I wouldn't shock me again if I were you. They're already pissed at you, and you'll just make your end worse." He pressed the side of his face to the partition. "Get the fucking glass already!"

The doctor slid the notebook into its carrying case sewn into the sleeve of his suit. He hesitated, looking at the sight of the man. Standing against the glass in his underwear, the patient looked less than human thanks to the varying black to purple skin shades.

Shaking his head, the doctor reached for the flexible aluminum arm, moving the magnifying glass into position. He flicked on the light, focusing it on the patient's face.

"Get on with it," the doctor said. "We have too much to do to be wasting time like this."

The man lifted away enough from the glass to bring up his hand. "Look at my eye. Look real close there, Doc." He pulled down the bottom lid, rolling his eye back into his head. Vibrating his hand slowly, he jiggled his face.

From the inside corner of the eye, by the tear duct, a pair of minute antennae emerged. The body of a louse followed, sticking for a moment beneath the lid before wiggling free. The parasite hesitated, apparently gaining its bearings, then scuttled down the patient's cheek. Another followed, and then a stream of the diminutive creatures, marching down the face like a living tear stream.

A drop of sweat slid into the doctor's eye. His legs went limp and wooziness filled his head. He turned off the light, swinging the magnifying glass away.

"Don't get all weak-kneed now, Doc." The patent stepped back from the glass, blinking. He smeared a hand across the cheek, examining what he'd wiped away. "I haven't told you about them crawling in my brain yet. You're going to love this shit."

Somehow, the doctor felt that he wasn't going to 'love this shit.'

"But let's digress, first. Has this all been worth it? I can't say so much that I blame you. If I thought I could control somebody completely, I would've considered doing it. And let's face it, Dr. Zimmerman was a hot tamale. Not to mention a freak in the bedroom. Wish I could have known her that way."

The doctor dropped the stylus. It bounced off the tile in the observation area.

"C'mon, Doc. You look stunned. Didn't you think I'd know this stuff?"

The doctor didn't answer.

"Never mind. Of course you didn't. You're little experiment didn't turn out exactly like you thought it would, did it? You can't control the lice, much less anybody else. Can you, Doc?"

"You don't know anything," the doctor said. "You're delusional."

"Oh, I know everything—all about your crazy plans and all about you, too. You're kind of a little freak yourself, aren't you? I mean, how much you like the finger up the ass when you're getting it on. Doc, that's kinda strange, there."

The doctor stepped back, falling into his chair. He missed the seat, landing on the plastic arm and bruising his tailbone.

"She knew you'd infected her on purpose, you know? Not a first, but when she was dying, she knew. Like I said, I can't blame you. You thought you could make her do anything. I mean, how could you resist?"

Overcoming the rush of thoughts pummeling him, the doctor pushed the intercom button. "You sir, have a very active imagination."

Patient 3442 cackled. It sounded like madness oozing through the speaker.

"I don't think the craziest fucker that ever lived could think up the shit I know. I know all about the technology you used. Brilliant really. Mapping living tissue with silicon chips so small they could fit into the body of a louse. If you weren't such a sick fuck, you'd be like, Nobel Prize-worthy."

The doctor pecked on the computer controlling the containment cell. The decontamination suit hindered his typing ability, and his hands shook with fear.

"Dr. Zimmerman thought she loved you, Phil. I guess considering the sick fuck you are, she'd have to. No other reason to help you with this insanity. But she did tell her friends about your 'issue.' You know, they have pills for that sort of thing. It happens to all of us now and again, but..."

Pounding furiously on the keyboard, the doctor enabled the initial sequence.

"Doc, don't you want to hear about when they get into your brain? That's when the magic happens."

The doctor backed away from the keyboard. He stumbled, falling to the tile.

"You see, they feed on your thoughts. But that's just the half of it. When they're in your head, you experience the thoughts—the memories—of their previous hosts. I never really met Dr. Zimmerman. Was just unfortunate enough to share a monorail car with her once. But I know everything about her—about you and her. All about your little project and its military funding. And how you failed, Phil."

The doctor blubbered. Picking himself up, he started the final sequence. The cyanide pill would drop into the small container of hydrochloric acid, creating a lethal gas, ending Patient 3442's life.

"That's not going to work, Doc. Like I said, I know everything. There's a keypad right here by the cell door. You installed it in case a staff member ever got locked in, right?"

Doctor Phil found the stylus to his notebook on the floor. Picking it up, he checked the rest of the observation area for anything important he might have left behind.

"Six." A high-pitched beep sounded through the speaker as the patient punched the number on the keypad.

The doctor went to the computer's keyboard. He hit 'enter.'

"Eight," the patient said. Another beep. "Two. Six. Three."

Drenched with sweat, the doctor removed his D-con suit helmet and pressed the intercom button. "Thank you for your time, sir. Good day."

"Star. Pound."

The cell door decompressed with the sound of

rushing air. The doctor dropped his notebook and froze. The odor of chemical baths and sweat invaded the observation room. The tiles turned black, lice sliding into the opening.

THE MADAM IN

ROOM 217

Two years to the day, Jonathan Keller returned to the Hotel De Paris in Georgetown. This time, alone, and with enough equipment to weigh down the VW bus so it never exceeded forty-five miles-per-hour up the mountain inclines. To be honest, though, it probably wouldn't have reached that speed without cargo. Even more honest, he had no idea how most of the equipment worked.

He limped around the two-story building upon arrival, taking more pictures than he'd need and shooting footage simply to delay going inside. The July sun was merciless. Sweat beaded on his brow, although most of that could be attributed to nerves. Jonathan confirmed the veranda's location, or the lack thereof. He recalled it on the west side, but as the police reports had confirmed, no veranda existed. Hadn't since the 1973 renovations according to the hotel manager's testimony, but even he couldn't explain the infamous photo.

Inside, the desk clerk remembered him. She shot Jonathan a look that called him every nasty name at once without uttering a word. "Returning to the scene of the crime, Mr. Keller?"

Jonathan put on his most charming smile, although it didn't work as well anymore. "My room ready?"

Somehow the crusty glare turned crustier. "I don't know why management agreed to this. Make it easier on everybody. Turn around. Crawl back under your rock in Hollywood."

"I gotta say, your attitude isn't doing much for your Yelp review."

"Does this help?" The woman, middle-aged, slightly chunky, bespectacled, and an apparent life-long employee shot out her middle finger and situated it inches from Jonathan's face.

"If I recall, the hotel reached out to us. I didn't ask for anything that followed. Truth be told, I'm the aggrieved party here."

"We didn't ask for what happened, either. Frankly, Mr. Keller, I'd prefer to forget you ever existed."

He smirked smugly and slipped his Master Card across the counter. "I'll be here all week. I'm sure your disposition will improve. I tend to grow on people."

"You start trouble again, you won't be here half a day." The clerk punished the computer keys with each stroke. She checked him in in silence, hatred simmering and seething, and slid the key card across the counter with such force, it spilled over the edge. "Room two-seventeen again. I trust you'll tote your bags yourself."

Jonathan picked the card from the floor, nodded at

the woman, and headed for the stairs. He whistled Bernard Herrmann's *Twisted Nerve* refrain, half to antagonize the clerk, half to calm himself. He paused at the staircase, inhaled and headed up, dragging his gimpy left foot over each step.

He thought he was ready to face what the hell had happened that night. At least, figure out what went down.

—

"You ever get tired of people hating you?" Lorelei set the camera atop its tripod. She peered through the viewer to catch a shirtless Jonathan gyrating in some exaggerated dance before the open second-floor window. His blond hair bounced, and his muscles rippled with every movement. He clutched a Budweiser tall-boy.

"They don't hate me—I'm one loveable SOB. They hate my character."

"Pretty sure it's you. Reality TV means you're the character." She clicked the record button, thinking the goofy dance would make fine footage for the episode's ending credits.

"They tuning in, though?"

"Hell yeah, they are."

"And don't the message boards call me 'Handsome Jack?'"

"Hell yeah, they do. And they're right, too."

"Then let them hate."

Lorelei joined her husband, she performing a

bastardized version of the Watusi.

"Shake it girl." Both clapped for musical accompaniment.

The heat inside the hotel room ratcheted a degree or three from the activity. Jonathan reached for her, rested his hands and beer can on her waist, and they broke into the box step, executing it as poorly as possible. It was a joke they'd shared since their dating days, and somehow it always crumpled them with laughter. When he went to kiss her, Lorelei thought: there goes the credits footage.

But before things got carried away, a knock rapped on the door. "Production meeting," Ernie yelled. "Room two-fourteen, five minutes."

"Five minutes." Jonathan raised his eyebrows in a playful gesture. "We could do it twice!"

"We'll be there," Lorelei shouted back as she pushed Jonathan away. She skipped to the door, undid the bolt and pulled on the knob. It didn't budge. "Very funny, Ernie. Let go."

No answer. She checked the peephole. No Ernie. She pulled the door again, but it wouldn't give. "Damn old hotels." More jiggling met with the same result. "You going to stand there looking pretty, or you gonna help me?" She jammed her shoulder into it a couple of times, but to no avail. The knob turned slippery as her hands sweat. The room's temperature had increased a few more degrees. "Jonathan?"

When she turned to see what the delay was, she

spotted him splayed across the bed. Not asleep, though. His body, glistened with sweat, vibrated. The bed rattled against the hardwood floor. The tall-boy spilled out on the mattress.

The camera, tripod and all, crashed to the hardwood. With a whoosh, the window slammed with enough force to create a crack through the pane's center.

Lorelei reached again for the door, but the knob burned her hand, and the scent of scorched flesh wafted. "Jonathan!" She sprinted for the bed and shook him by the shoulder with her uninjured hand. His eyes had rolled back, and foam dribbled from his mouth. "Baby!" She cocked her arm to slap him.

Before she could deliver the blow, he shot straight up, eyes returning. The bed ceased shaking. The door opened. The temperature dropped a good ten degrees.

"What the hell happened?" Jonathan asked.

Lorelei inspected her co-star, searching for any hints on his face. Her heart thundered with such force she heard it pulse through her head. "You do that?"

Jonathan shook his head. He gulped breaths as if trying to recover from a strenuous run.

"How'd you do that with the doorknob?" She displayed her hand and pointed to the small blister forming in her left palm. "We need some footage of this."

Another rap on the door. Ernie leaned inside. "Let's go, Kellers. Time is money, and I ain't got enough of either."

"You're getting really good at this, Baby" she said to Jonathan. "This is going to rock."

—

Despite the clerk's refusal to assist him, Jonathan had tracked down a porter who'd delivered his equipment to room 217. Except for the duffle bag of champagne bottles. Jonathan had lugged that himself, preferring not to have to answer for them. The sole condition, besides the exorbitant fee, management had stipulated was Jonathan couldn't drink this visit. A condition he intended to honor, but still didn't want to explain how the champagne wasn't for him.

Now, on his third day locked in the room 217, the champagne taunted. He'd kept a couple of bottles on ice in case his visitor ever showed herself.

His mind messed with him, as well. Each noise, he assigned some otherworldly explanation, but he didn't know if they originated from Lorelei or Mattie Silks, or maybe Handsome Jack Ready himself. In the end, most simply were the result of his mind going batty with boredom.

"Maybe I just don't remember things properly," he said into the camera. He'd purposely allowed his stubble to sprout and hadn't touched his hair. Thought it made him gritty and the scene more intense. He spoke in hushed tones for dramatic effect. "Maybe I...Maybe it was just the crew messing around and things got out of hand."

He looked over both shoulders, then leaned into the camera. "Confession time: Most of the things you saw on Keller's Paranormal Journal...well...to put it nicely, they were fabricated. We lived by one rule—the 'Any Rule.' Any crew member could set up any stunt at any time and not tell anybody. Maybe the crew rigged everything that night and they've hushed so not to go through what I did.

"Lorelei encouraged them to scare us. The worse the scare, the better the TV, and she would have killed to make good TV." He tried forcing a tear, but couldn't. Thoughts of Lorelei only brought numbness now, and he'd cried himself out while in jail. "Instead, she died trying to make good TV."

He clicked off the record button and cursed under his breath for being melodramatic, reconciled he needed to be. With no network backing, his little YouTube channel was his only path for a comeback. He'd blown the rest of Lorelei's life insurance cash on this excursion. No longer able to rely on effects, he needed to make himself the center of everything. Which was fine—he always thought himself the star of the show anyhow.

Hitting record again, he walked the camcorder to the instruments. "The EMF meter shows nothing. Still. Two days and not a single instrument has registered squat."

He turned the camera to himself. "I'm running out of time to clear myself. At least in the court of public opinion. Something better happen soon, or this will make me look worse." He stopped recording and wondered what he could do next.

Photographs spread across the desk table, arranged in the most striking manner possible. Taking a few seconds on each photo, he zoomed in for a close-up on the most pertinent to his 'investigation.'

"This is Mattie Silks, infamous madam. Funny how beauty standards change over time. This plump harlot was considered one of the most beautiful women of the old west. And, romanticizing aside, a cold-hearted businessperson."

He caught a drop of sweat before it sullied the photos. "This here, is the famous photo from my trial. As you can clearly see, a veranda did indeed exist on the second-floor's west side. No other photo we took showed this, but clearly it's there." Jonathan cleared his throat. "Over ten experts at the trial testified this photo was not doctored, and not one could explain the veranda."

Jonathan stopped before focusing on the most famous photo, though. He'd cross that bridge later—as late as possible—and would dread facing it every second until his week concluded. Setting the camera aside, he sat on the unmade bed.

The room wasn't as hot as he'd remembered, but sweat still soaked his Ghostbusters t-shirt. The ceiling fan hadn't worked two years ago, and apparently the maintenance staff was as committed as the wench at the front desk. The fan taunted Jonathan as he lay back. He reached into the ice bucket, fished out half-melted cubes from the water and rubbed them over his forehead. Unconsciously, he found his hand back in the bucket, grasping a bottle.

When he realized this, he jolted from the bed. Camera in tow, he strode to the door. It opened easily—to his disappointment.

The hallway was much more comfortable, the air conditioning functioning there. Still, Jonathan's chest tightened every time he entered the corridor. He swallowed a breath, hit record, and began what would probably be the most difficult segment of the episode. The window on the west end of the hall came into focus. The new paint didn't quite match to the wall surrounding the replaced window. He struggled keeping the frame from shaking. He thought he could write that off to his limp, but his trembling hands accounted for the majority.

"And here's where it all happened."

———

Ernie handed out the script to the usual unruly, surly comments from the four-person crew. Jonathan and Lorelei entered room 214 to these familiar jeers. Jonathan carried a six pack and bottle of Makers Mark. Lorelei brought a smartass grin and a command of the room.

"Quiet down, degenerates. We're here for three days, but if we wrap this in two, the network would be elated." Ernie spoke like somebody ten years older, although Lorelei could never pin down his exact age. He shaved his head, and his dark skin offered no wrinkles. A beer gut hung over his belt, but his arms were large and firm. His entire wardrobe consisted of Levi's and white t-shirts. "Time is money—"

"And you ain't got enough of either," the group answered in unison.

Jonathan dealt the beers and opened the bottle. Lorelei had noticed this becoming more of a ritual than she felt comfortable with, but understood the stress of the show incited a lot of the behavior. After the season, she vowed, she'd sit down with her husband for a long talk about all of the mess.

"We're going to focus on Mattie Silks and Handsome Jack Ready." Ernie popped his beer top. "She was a madam in several towns across the old west, and he was a prick."

"Sounds about right," Lorelei said.

"In the eighteen-seventies, she operated a brothel across town, but special clients were brought to the Hotel De Paris. Some stories say these clients were never seen again."

"Ooooh," Justin, the camera operator, said in his ghostliest voice. Ernie's nephew, he sported an afro straight out of a Pam Grier movie and spent the majority of his waking hours sharing quality time with his good friend, Mr. Cannabis.

"The hotel wants to play up on the haunted thing

to bring in more business, so anything goes, got me?" Ernie continued. "As far as they and we are concerned, Mattie Silks still operates in this hotel—specifically room two-seventeen."

Lorelei stood and positioned herself next to Ernie. "If y'all keep up what you've started, we're going to do right by the Hotel De Paris. I'm sure we've got some usable content already." She popped open her beer. "Anybody want to take credit for that doorknob? You heat it from the outside?"

The crew looked around to each other. Nobody would take credit. That was the game.

"Let's be a little careful with that stuff." She held her hand to show off the blister. "I don't mind giving a little skin for my art, but this shit hurts."

"Nice!" Ernie said. "That's what we're looking for."

"Got it. Burn Lorelei," Travis said in his nerdy-chic way. His title was co-producer, but it meant he did everything nobody else wanted to do.

"All right. Should be dark in three hours. Get whatever interviews you need while Trav hooks up the room."

"Finishes hooking up the room," Lorelei added.

"I ain't been in there, Mrs. Keller. I'd take credit for it, but I can't."

Ernie polished off his beer in a single, long chugging drink. "Nine p.m.—room two-seventeen. Be there, on time, so we can meet our deadline."

Jonathan stood, put his hand out and called the

crew to bring it in. "Keller Paranormal Journal on three," he said. "One, two..."

"Fuck you," the crew called as a choir.

———

Jonathan must have passed out after the second bottle of champagne. Coming to, his tongue occupied his entire mouth and had grown a fur coat that tasted of sour ass. He reached into the ice bucket and scooped out a couple of handfuls of water, the cold liquid the perfect antidote for his parched palette.

Sweat glued him to the mattress. His vision took far too long to focus, but when it did, he still couldn't identify what appeared out of place. When he finally figured it out, it wasn't so much the visual as the sound that gave it away—a rhythmic ticking. Dare he hope—a haunted ticking?

From his prone position, he noticed the ceiling fan blades whirling, propelling hot air throughout the narrow room. His stomach lurched when he bolted from the bed. The EMF meter, which read electromagnetic activity, went ballistic.

"Come out, you bitch." He searched the room for the camera. "That you, Mattie? Happy to see me again?"

The fan twirled faster. Jonathan was so caught up in the activity, it didn't occur to him he had zero idea how to communicate with an actual ghost. He fought back the dry heaves and dizziness and hit record.

The camcorder engaged. He zoomed in on the fan.

"Day three. Mattie Silks makes an appearance." Adrenaline rushed, forcing alcohol through his veins faster. He directed the shot at the EMF meter. "Clearly, I am not alone. Come out, Mattie. Come out and play."

Despite the confidence he tried projecting, he felt officially freaked. Lorelei had always been the planner of the two. As usual, Jonathan flew by the seat of his shorts, and properly (metaphorically) soiled shorts at that.

His taunts garnered no response, though. He whistled the *Twisted Nerve* melody again until he grew bored. The meter danced, the fan whirled, but other than the room warming, nothing else. For hours. Jonathan chilled another champagne bottle— champagne was allegedly Mattie Silks drink of choice— in the melted ice. Waited for a sign. Listened to the annoying ticking of the chains hanging from the unbalanced ceiling fan. The pattern of the clicks should have been rhythmic, he thought, but they sounded in bursts.

About the time he thought of opening the bottle, thinking a bit of the hair of the dog might calm his queasiness, it finally hit him.

The sounds registered in no pattern after all. They were Morse Code.

—

Around midnight, to escape the heat of room 217 and a disappointing night of failures, Lorelei and Jonathan snuck to the window located at the west end of the hall and shared a cigarette.

"You think Travis is toking with Justin or something?" Lorelei asked. "It's not like him to fuck up this bad."

"Maybe he shot his wad with that doorknob trick."

"But the whole crew?" She accepted the Virginia Slim from him. "We better figure out something quick. I don't care how good these guys are at editing—we're in some trouble here."

"We got two more days."

"Bullshit. When Ernie says the network prefers two days, we have a day and a half." Lorelei's stomach tumbled onto itself. She hadn't shared the latest ratings. This would be their last season unless the finale pulled off something spectacular, but saw no purpose in stressing Jonathan.

"Hey! There's no smoking in here." The desk clerk stomped up the garish corridor carpet that looked like Timothy Leary had vomited an LSD dream all over it. She slowed as she neared, though. "Oh. Mr. and Mrs. Keller. I didn't realize—"

"We're sorry." Jonathan dialed up smile number ten and Lorelei knew they could have been smoking crack with naked eight-year-olds—Jonathan was going to charm their way out. "It's just the altitude. We were worried about making it back up them steps again, ma'am. Can you forgive us this one time? Perhaps you'd join us?"

The woman actually blushed. Lorelei thought she

smelled the clerk lubricating her granny panties. Handsome Jack at work.

"I don't smoke. If you two could just open the window, I'll let it slide this time. But if any guests object, I'll have to ask you to stop. Fair?"

"More than, ma'am. You folks are right friendly around here. We appreciate you putting up with our silliness."

"Nonsense, Jack. It's an honor to have you."

"Thank you." Jonathan turned his smile to eleven. "We'll mosey off to bed after finishing up this nasty thing. Sorry we had to bother you."

The woman pivoted and waddled down the hall, an extra giddy-up in her step.

"I think she wants you, Handsome Jack."

"Well, she's only flesh and blood."

"Us poor mortals." Lorelei opened the window further. "How about we finish this outside?"

"What?"

"There's a walkway out there."

"Since when?"

Lorelei wrapped the thin blanket around her. "Dunno. Since Mattie Silks pimped out bitches to silver miners under the nose of her husband, Handsome Jack? Let's get some fresh air." She stepped through the window and onto the veranda. "Your girlfriend, the desk clerk, won't bother us out here."

"I'll be damned." Jonathan grabbed his mostly empty bottle of Makers Mark and joined his wife.

She immediately regretted it. Once Jonathan joined her, the veranda didn't feel as substantial. Somehow, the blanket about her seemed suffocating, and she swore the temperature soared.

Jonathan took no notice though. He pounded the rest of the bottle, then grinned like the Cheshire Cat on pain killers. No way he could have seen the orb over his shoulder.

Reaching for her camera, excitement overwhelmed her, and Lorelei failed in forming a full sentence.

"What is it, Babe?"

The orb expanded, drew close enough to her husband, it blurred his face.

"It's Mattie Silks." Lorelei noted Jonathan's laughter moments before the window slammed shut. It trapped the straggling blanket. The orb flashed in a blinding burst, then fled. The veranda collapsed. Disappeared. Lorelei understood her fate before her neck snapped.

—

Jonathan typed out the coded messages on his laptop. It'd been a few years since Boy Scouts, so he wasn't sure he transcribed everything perfectly, but he got the gist.

She's with me, Jack.

You can see her.

Can you forgive me? I got confused about Handsome Jack.

She's a good worker. A good earner.

She misses you.

She's mad you left her to be a whore.

Jonathan had positioned the camera behind him and the laptop's Skype camera was also recording. He didn't know what point he should cut them off, but thought one of them would finally catch him sobbing— the money shot.

You can be with her.

For a price. Whores need to be paid, Handsome Jack. Only sluts work for free.

The room had to be over a hundred degrees. Jonathan sweat out the three bottles of champagne and then some. He pounded out Morse Code on the table. *Why? Why her.*

It wasn't her. It was you.

He knocked more, as best his drunken mind could recall. *Let me see her.*

What do you have to offer, Jack?

He bit back the vomit gorging in his throat. *What would it take?* he asked in a series of dots and dashes.

The fan slowed. Stopped for a moment.

"No!" Jonathan screamed. "Let me see her."

With a new energy, the fan recommenced its swirling. Ferociously, as if it might break free from the ceiling and fly away of its own volition.

I want to feel flesh again.

I want to be alive.

I need a vessel.

Jonathan rapped on the table, each knock sounding wet from the blood bursting via his knuckles.

What vessel? What's a vessel?

Give me your body, and your soul can be with her.

"Jonathan." Lorelei's voice. Faint, but unmistakable. It emanated from the Shack Hack—a radio the show had used dozens of times to mimic a ghost's voice. "Don't leave me here, Baby. I can't do this."

He no longer needed to pretend to cry. "Lor? That you?"

A body. I need a body if you want to be with her.

You prepared for this, Handsome Jack?

Help me, Jonathan. It's awful.

Jonathan knocked in code again: *A body? Any body?*

Any body.

"Jonathan, I miss you."

He stood from the desk and paced the room. Sweat fell off him in sheets and champagne clouded his brain.

She was pregnant, Jack. You know that?

Jonathan went to the duffle bag and popped open a warm bottle. The alcohol rushed through the opening, spilled onto the floor, and he put his mouth over the gusher, letting it all in.

Give me a minute, he knocked. After walking over to the phone, he dialed the front desk.

"You ready to leave, Mr. Keller?" the bitchy voice asked.

"Yes. Please help me with my bags."

"I'll send somebody."

"I'd prefer you. I owe you an apology."

A moment of silence. "Fine. I'll be there momentarily."

He hung up. He rapped on the desk. *I got you a body. I want my wife.*

DEAD QUIET

Late Friday afternoon:

The black Cadillac with bullet-proof windows and US Government license plates pulled into the horseshoe-shaped, gravel driveway. The marshal killed the engine and popped the trunk.

"You're some kinda hero, ain't you, Mr. Henderson?" The marshal's drawl was thick and unplaceable, like an amateur actor trying on a southern persona.

Myles met the driver's eyes in the rearview mirror. "According to the two whole people on the internet who seem to care, I'm nothing but a rat."

"I believe that term is more in parlance with greasy mafia types, not government whistleblowers such as yourself."

"Like they're not the same."

"Rats," the marshal said, "are a lower lifeform."

"I meant between the government and the mafia." Myles pulled the handle, but the door wouldn't budge.

"There's definitely a difference." The marshal unlocked the back door. "The mafia operates on an honor code."

Mountain air, thin, humid and heated by summer, punched Myles in the lungs. He met the marshal at the opened trunk. After a few awkward moments, Myles lifted his palms, shrugged his shoulders.

"I ain't your valet, Mr. Henderson. Schlep your own damn bags."

Inside the cabin, the marshal opened the kitchen window and stomped spiders either too lazy to scurry or too brave for their own good. "I don't know what you're gonna tell that grand jury, Mr. Henderson, but if the senator is hiding you here, I know you're in danger, young man."

"Ya think?" Myles dropped his suitcase in the foyer as he accepted the moment—almost allowed pride, but his underlying fear kept that sin in check.

"Cell." The marshal presented his hand and clapped his fingers to the palm.

Myles responded with a confused expression.

"Your phone. There ain't any service out here any old ways, but we can't risk the chance of somebody tracing you."

After losing a stare down, Myles surrendered his iPhone. "What if there's an emergency?"

"See that there's not." The marshal checked the various light switches and made sure the fridge hadn't shat its bed. "You have enough food for the weekend. Ain't exactly The French Laundry, but there's a grill out back and enough beer to keep you numb. Hope you ain't vegan."

Myles opened his immaculate pressed suit jacket, pushed aside the pristine paisley tie and rubbed his taught belly. "This look vegan to you?"

"I didn't have that impression. Don't stay outside

too long. See any drones, get back in the cabin right quick and lock the doors—but only after you've put out the grill. It's fire season."

They examined the abode. Natural wood dominated the interior except for a stone fireplace. The dwelling appeared as solid as the mountain that housed it. Echoes should have been an issue.

After a checklist Myles paid less than no attention to, the marshal handed him the tv remote. "You can't get any stations, but the ottoman's full of VHS tapes to kill the time. Blu-Ray is still outside the department's budget." The marshal led him back to the kitchen. "The library is well stocked, and you got the three-day weekend to review your statement. We'll be back before you go completely nutso."

"Promise?"

"No." There was no joking in the marshal's poor accent.

"What's the wi-fi password?"

"Got a pen?" The marshal lit a cigarette, a long thin one with an almost black wrapper. "Write this down: go fuck yourself." He inhaled another drag and blew the plume direct into Myles' face. "No internet, no phone, no way we lose your bean-counting ass before Monday, Mr. Henderson. Your testimony is making the Beltway very uncomfortable. Our job is to protect you from any adverse entities, including your own damn self."

"Somebody's uncomfortable, huh? Couldn't tell from the news channels. I haven't seen squat about this case."

"Yes. And you're welcome." The marshal held the cigarette like a joint and inhaled again. "Don't worry. Come Monday afternoon, you'll wish nobody'd ever heard of you."

Myles gritted his teeth and nodded. He thought there was one person he wanted to have heard of him. "Why's the senator leaving me out here alone? I'm so goddamned important, shouldn't I have protection?"

"It's only two-and-a-half days. We don't want to leave a car in the driveway and attract attention."

"But no bodyguard?"

The marshal rubbed out the cigarette on his shoe's sole before returning the unsmoked portion to the pack. "In your position, knowing what you know, would you trust being left alone with anybody else? In the wilderness, your mind pulls some crazy tricks, Mr. Henderson. We'd prefer not to stoke any unneeded paranoia by stationing somebody at your door."

Myles decided it best to not push the matter. There was no changing the situation at that point.

"You've got everything you need," the marshal said. "I've never lost anybody from this location yet."

The statement mildly stunned Myles. He hadn't considered ever being 'lost.'

The marshal grabbed a Heineken from the fridge, tipped it to his forehead like a salute before he popped the bottle open, and exited the cabin. The door slammed as loud as an explosion.

—

Myles listened for the Caddie to drive away, but heard no engine, no crushed gravel, not a hint of gears shifting. He checked through the front drapes and confirmed the marshal had left. Living in DC for the past decade, Myles had grown accustomed to traffic and sirens and protest chants and arguments in any and every language creating the general hubbub of a major city.

The new-found quiet was, well, disquieting.

Myles sat at the lacquered picnic table in the dining room and grasped the zipper of the laptop bag. He expected opening the case to be loud as a lion's roar, but the zipper teeth separated as if they'd come to a peaceful understanding.

Maybe one of them beers wasn't such a bad idea.

After retrieving a bottle and powering up his HP, arranging his pens by color and notebooks by sizes, he opened the familiar file: Memoir.

To his disappointment, it hadn't magically grown past the first two paragraphs he'd written over and again during the past six months:

Chapter one—Your government is cheating you. I know because Senator McLaughlin hired me to see if I could find any discrepancies in the defense budget. And, Lordy, they're there. Thing is, upon reflection and for reasons you shall soon read, I think the honorable senator didn't have the best intentions of our great country as his major motivation. I think he wanted me to find any flaws in his plans.

My name is Myles Henderson. I'm what you might call a super accountant. The following events are one-hundred percent true and will one-hundred percent blow your ever-loving mind.

Myles highlighted the entire section and deleted it. He retyped the words from memory, hoping they'd create momentum—the rhythm from keys tapping would provide a bass beat result in page after page of bonafide bestseller. Or at least an end product that'd sell enough to cover a couple months' worth of alimony payments. And show Sheila she quit on him too early.

But the keys didn't click nor clack, and words didn't stick nor stack. One beer led to another and another, and sooner than he thought possible, night captured the mountain.

After dining on a ham sandwich and his eighth beer, he peeled off his suit, hung it neatly on a hanger, and folded his shirt and underclothes before placing them in the designated dirty laundry bag. He then stumbled to the bedroom. His footfalls landed without resonance. The mattress proved far too soft. The springs released no groans or creaks.

Myles belched, if only for the company, but the room swallowed the emission and it barely registered. He snuggled with a pillow. Out of habit, he smelled, but the foreign linen held no lingering memory of Sheila.

He contemplated fetching her perfume he'd stashed in his luggage but was too drunk to follow through.

Silence weighed as immense as the forest outside, and Myles sensed each sheltered countless unwelcome creatures. Despite his substantial buzz, the sandman stayed far away. Sweat poured off Myles. Convinced he'd find some measure of comfort, he opened the bedroom window. The screech echoed through the canyon. Running down his spine, it raised goose pimples on his neck. Surely, it couldn't be as loud as he'd heard.

"Hello?" he yelled. The exclamation disappeared into the night, not allowing even the courtesy of an echo.

Disturbed, thinking he must be more drunk than he'd realized, Myles lay back down. He strained his ears—not even a cricket. Thoughts looped in his mind, gaining speed with each spin before focusing on a memory of an article he'd read. The story had centered on the quietest room on record. The writer had claimed, thanks to the insulation in the anechoic chamber, nobody could remain inside for an hour without slipping into insanity. The room actually registered in negative decibels.

As he contemplated such a space, the wind kicked up outside. Myles exhaled a breath he'd been unaware of holding. Of course, he heard nothing upon its release.

The breeze stirred leaves. It whistled softly

through spaces between trees. Despite the welcome cooling, it provided little comfort. An ominous tone trailed in its wake.

Myles squeezed his eyes shut like he could will himself entrance into Slumberland's gates.

The whispers the wind carried coalesced. Some unfamiliar, yet distinct, language formed words in a disembodied, unsettling female voice. As low in volume as they were, they still punished his ears. The gusts gathered strength. More feminine voices joined and created an inhuman choir. Their hymn made no sense, but the malevolent tone hummed through Myles' bones.

Scrambling from the bed, he slammed the window shut. It didn't squeal this time. The windows rattled silently as the wind gained momentum and shook the cabin.

Myles wrapped himself in the comforter and headed for the front room. He sat at the picnic table, the peace oppressive and relentless, and watched outside. He didn't fall asleep until after dawn.

——

Late Saturday morning:

Hornets buzzed inside his head. His stomach tumbled. The quart of orange juice he'd guzzled hadn't hydrated him, and his thoughts moved like blobs through a lava lamp.

At least a dozen times he'd searched the cabin for his phone, panicked he might have drunk-dialed Sheila.

Finally, he'd written himself a note to remember the feds had it. When he thought of it like that, his gut churned with more force.

Making things worse, the cursor on the screen taunted him.

He'd teased himself with several third paragraphs but erased them each before their completion. By eleven, he decided the hair of the dog might be his only cure. It didn't take away the hangover, but he felt better after beer number three.

Ringing in his head provided a semblance of white noise. The void of sound, he told himself, wasn't as bad as it'd been in the dead of night. Daylight brought new perspective, yet no answers. Was the mountainside always so unnaturally quiet? It felt as if the cabin actively swallowed sound—like it was silencing him.

Myles closed the laptop, cursor still waiting for a third paragraph. After finding some fruit in the fridge, he made his way to the television room. He popped a couple of the grapes in his mouth as he studied the large, narcissistic portrait of Senator McLaughlin that covered most of the back wall. Contained in a gauche, ornate gold frame, the painting depicted the senator from his first term, some forty years before. Fifty pounds lighter and still some remnants of a hairline intact, the permanent smug expression graced the senator's face. Myles formed his hand into a finger gun and fired. I got you, he thought. You sonofabitch, I got you.

He retired to the worn pleather couch, opened the ottoman and searched through the videos—sixties westerns, Ken Burns' documentaries, and the entire run of *Green Acres*. Taking them out, he spread the tapes across the couch and began arranging them in alphabetical order. Nothing spoke to him as a must-see, but it kept his mind off the strange cabin, the grand jury, and Sheila.

Well, not completely off his soon-to-be ex-wife—the state of their relationship consistently followed him, a dark cloud of failure and missed opportunities. He allowed a moment of fantasy. Of her seeing him swarmed by a mass of press, grasping how important he'd become. Then, he realized his fantasies used to be much more exciting.

Once he started returning the tapes—in proper order—back to their storage, he noticed a bump in the ottoman's compartment. A layer of beige shelf paper covered the bottom. One corner was raised. Myles peeled back the paper to find an unmarked tape. His mind went to a porno. Why else would it be hidden and with no label? He decided he warranted a little relaxation and could kill a good three or four minutes.

He pressed the ancient VCR's play button. Quickly, he realized it was no porn movie. The man in the frame wasn't familiar, but the setting was. Behind the black man with bloodshot eyes who donned an impeccable suit, the portrait of Senator McLaughlin hung.

"Fuck me," Myles mouthed.

His heart thundered. For a moment, he thought he might throw up as realizations hit him.

"I am Alonzo Perriman." The voice hurt Myles' ears. Using the remote, he turned down the volume, but noticed it was only on three.

"I've been a private contractor for Senator McLaughlin for the past few months, working on a secret project. I'm an accountant by trade, and the senator hired me to review budget irregularities of the Defense Department." It became clear the man in the video was yelling. "The senator is the ranking member of his party on the Appropriations Committee and serves in a senior position on the Armed Services Committee."

Myles paused the video. His thoughts couldn't keep up. After catching his breath, he re-started, knowing he wasn't ready to hear what came next.

"During my review, I quickly realized the senator hadn't been forthright with me." Perriman's voice wasn't as loud, although he still yelled his words. Myles upped the volume to six. "In many instances, I discovered inconsistencies, and upon further investigation, found the senator and/or his donors were financially benefiting from these anomalies."

The sound kept diminishing. Myles cranked the TV to maximum volume.

"I believe the senator has been using my work to find ways to cover his tracks. I intended to testify as such before a grand jury on Monday, June fifth, two-thousand-six."

The man clearly screamed at this point, but the sound lessened with each word. "If you've found this tape, you're most likely aware of what I'm talking about. I now know I won't be testifying. I realized they wouldn't have driven me to a top-secret location without blindfolding me unless they never intended—"

The audio stopped. Perriman continued yelling into the camera, veins bulging from his neck.

Myles scurried from the couch and put his ear against the television speaker. It proved a fruitless effort.

The tape continued for another few minutes. Perriman grew visibly more distraught with each second. Spittle covered the lens. Specks of blood soon added to the mess. The video ended with him in tears.

Myles turned off the television. Senator McLaughlin's portrait, smug expression and all, glared at him.

—

Late Saturday night:

His wrists ached from typing. It wasn't the book he'd envisioned, but Myles detailed everything he remembered, and he possessed an elephant's memory. He left directions on where the senator hid evidence. He listed violations. Every time he thought he'd finished, he recalled more. Typos littered the document, but anybody who would uncover it could nail the senator and his committees.

Before closing the laptop, he went to the first page. Above the title he wrote: *For Sheila. Always.*

He took a breath and finally recognized the time. No sound escaped when he closed the laptop. The silence stalked him like a boogeyman growing closer every moment.

The windows vibrated from the haunting wind.

Adrenaline wouldn't allow Myles any sleep. In the darkness, he sat, again wrapped in the comforter, on the couch and gazed into the night. He couldn't believe how many stars decorated the sky. He sung himself Beatles' songs. The vibrations from his voice box tickled his throat, but none of the soundwaves made it to his ears.

As the hours ticked by, and Myles faced a final full day and night before rescue, his silent screams started hurting his throat. He again recalled the article on the anechoic chamber and wondered if he'd lost his sanity. Unable to endure the quiet any longer, he crept to the window. He sobbed as he opened it to the wind.

The chorus sang in rounds, lyrics of unrelated syllables that absolutely meant something yet nothing. Myles couldn't discern if their song was beautiful, or just hearing anything provided him some relief.

Around two in the morning, Myles noticed the pattern. He couldn't decipher it mentally, but it spoke to his soul. It didn't provide any comfort.

He dressed, packed his laptop, and escaped into the woods, following the voices.

—

Next Friday, late afternoon:

The black Cadillac with bullet-proof windows and US Government license plates pulled into the horseshoe-shaped, gravel driveway. The marshal killed the engine and popped the trunk.

"You're some kinda hero, ain't you, Ms. Simmons?" The marshal's drawl was thick and unplaceable, like an amateur actor trying on a southern persona.

CONTINUATION 2020

Trinity stands next to the half-dead ash tree in the front yard, arms folded, fingernails digging into her ribs. Mom keeps talking, trying to make it better, like she always does. Trinity loves her for that, but it gets old. The dress her parents forced her to wear is too tight. They think they're making her feel better by buying smaller sizes, but it doesn't work. It's embarrassing.

The horns sound down Rouge Avenue. Grow louder. Her anxiety reaches an eight. She tastes the stomach acid in the back of her throat and wishes she could escape her own skin.

Her Inner-she's screams are deafening in her mind.

"Here they come, Punkin." Nerves vibrate in Mom's voice. Trinity wishes she could calm her and let her know what to expect. Trinity's used to it now. Almost.

Louder horns, and now voices and car stereos sound out. *High Hopes* by Panic at the Disco beats through the neighborhood, and Trinity allows a moment to bob her head along. Like she could belong. Be normal like everybody else.

Her heart thuds. She hears the blood rush through her head. She's slightly woozy. This is it, she thinks.

But the parade stays on Rouge. Nobody waves at

her. Nobody except Dad from his ancient PT Cruiser.

"Bon voyage," he yells. "Don't forget to write. Have a safe trip. Don't forget to write. We'll miss you. Bon voy-ah-gee."

Dad's a dork.

Trinity's knees shake. She doesn't want to be here at all, but now Mom feels sorry for her. "It's a big day" Mom said that morning. "We're going to celebrate like one," Dad added.

Inner-she's rage burned.

"Don't worry, Punkin. They're coming back around." Mom kneads Trinity's shoulders. Her touch, too tight, not right, betrays the confidence in her words.

The last car in the convoy is a Tesla. 2020 EIGHTH GRADE is painted on its windows, almost a taunt, tin cans tag behind. Trinity's stomach tumbles as a ball forms in her thick midsection. It's him. And, true to form, Khalil sees Trinity. He presents a double middle-finger salute and laughs. And laughs. And laughs.

Mom pretends not to notice. For Mom's sake, Trinity pretends, too. But her mind's awash in the awful memories of that jerk. From kindergarten through eighth grade, his one mission appeared to be to ruin Trinity's life. From sticking her with the Trinity Infinity moniker, a dig at her weight, to stealing her Gameboy Advance in third grade—an act she still hadn't told Mom or Dad about because she wasn't supposed to take it to school. Just seeing Khalil in the halls brought on anxiety attacks. When puberty hit, he only grew worse.

Inner-she bathes in well-rehearsed revenge fantasies. Uses the blood as moisturizer. The devil's aloe.

Music fades. Voices drive out of range. Horns sound a gagillion miles away. Trinity's heart sinks. She's not sure she can maintain for Mom. Anxiety might win this one. She can't breathe. She can't move.

Inner-she hopes the ash tree falls on her and Trinity.

Seconds before Trinity crumbles, horns grow louder again. Hope fills Mom's laugh. Despite her instincts, optimism swells in Trinity's spirit. Middle school was bad enough, so the quarantine suits her fine. She misses her few friends, but they haven't called much since lockdown began. Now with it over, she won't create any new opportunities to embarrass herself thanks to the 'virtual' continuation. Maybe it'd be the sendoff she needed to start her summer—a break from the parents' questions about social life and grades and 'boyfriends?' Maybe this time it'll work out like it did for other kids. That had to happen sooner or later, right?

Inner-she reminds her it hasn't happened yet. Why start now?

Horns honk. Passengers holler. Only seven cars remain as the parade winds down 25th Place. Trinity bites her tongue so not to cry.

Dad continues with his same crappola: "Bon voy-ah-gee. Don't forget to write." It's still not funny but at least he's making a fool of himself. Perhaps taking a little of the attention off her.

The final car is still the Tesla. This time Khalil rubs his butt cheeks against the window. Mom again pretends not to notice and blows kisses at Dad. Another inch of Trinity's soul dies and she curses the ash tree for not falling and the lawn for not opening up and swallowing her.

Inner-she pictures running after the Tesla, dragging her bully out and bashing his head into the asphalt until he apologizes for everything.

A golden retriever puppy pops up next to Khalil and yaps. Another one? Trinity thinks. They must own a hundred dogs. Every week, it seemed they had a new puppy.

Later, Trinity's family poses for photos she'll never want seen, but both grandmothers will post on their Facebook pages and tag her. All 18 of Trinity's Facebook friends will see them. She loathes Facebook and avoids Insta and Tik Tok altogether. She only has a FB page because her grandparents wanted to keep in touch and feel hip. Mascara streams down her face and stains the too-tight, too-awful, fuchsia dress. At least it gives an excuse to change her clothes.

———

After bedtime, Mom enters her room. Trinity puts on her best brave face and sets her organ keyboard on the floor. She doesn't want to be a burden but can't face Mom. She sits on the bed's edge, facing the wall. Mom sits on the other side. She rubs Trinity's back, but Trinity can only think of all the blubber Mom massages.

"I'm proud of you, Punkin. I know it was hard, but you made it." Mom lies down and cuddles around her, resting an arm over Trinity's belly. "The worst is over. I promise. You're gonna have a good life because you deserve it."

"That's a pretty big promise, Mama-san."

Inner-she resents Mom for perpetuating such a myth.

Mom forces a laugh that is both understanding and uncomfortable. "He's going to a different high school. You'll probably never see him again. So yes, Punkin, the worst is over."

Mom gets out of the bed and kneels beside Trinity. "Remember, Sweetie, for him to be that awful of a person in public, something terrible is happening to him in private. Be the bigger person and move on. Otherwise, you'll never find happiness."

Inner-she prays something terrible happens to Khalil in private. Like he sleeps on a bed of ants and his blanket is filled with spikes and honey.

"I think he's just a psychopath." Trinity lies down and pulls the Princess Leia comforter over her. While the quiet time is nice, she hopes Mom leaves before the requisite ceremonial nightly crying spell.

122 / SAM W. ANDERSON

Inner-she knows despite Mom's reassurances, the worst is probably yet to come. Minus yet.

Dad enters. "They say it's your continuation," he sings. "It's my continuation, too!" He plays air guitar and sings the refrain again.

Dad's a dork.

He places something on Trinity's temple and sings another round of the stupid refrain. She takes the package from her head and sits up against her headboard. It's wrapped in rainbow-patterned paper."

"Thanks, Papa-san."

"That's from both of us. And remember the card I showed you? We mean that, too." Mom and Dad agreed years ago to stop exchanging greeting cards. Instead, they'd go to the Kroger's, look through the selection and share the one they thought best expressed their feelings. No need to waste money on the card when the sentiment what's important, right? Trinity still wanted the card, though.

She rips open the paper to reveal the iPhone 11 box. Trinity would never have imagined asking for such an expensive gift. For a moment, she couldn't form words. Maybe things are going to be different?

"We're trusting you with this," Dad says. "You need to be mature about it. No more missing Gameboy incidents, okay?"

Inner-she says aloud in her head, "Things aren't going to be different."

Trinity doles out mandatory hugs and thank-yous

and instantly falls in love with her gift. Normal teenagers have this, she thinks. Maybe it's the tool she needs. Maybe it's the chance for others to see her in a different light.

She spends the night downloading her info from the Cloud.

———

Mom wants to bake cookies for a break in the monotony. She sends Trinity to Kroger's, mask in place and hand sanitizer in tow.

The first weeks of summer break were fine, but three weeks in, Trinity welcomes the escape opportunity.

She waits outside the grocery on the designated tape lines. The mask, homemade by Mom with Star Wars-themed pattern, hinders her hot breath, and Trinity smells lunch's ham sandwich.

From five spots back, she hears the voice. She nearly melts in place. "Infinity? That you?"

Achieved: Level nine on anxiety ladder. For a moment she hops out of line and starts back home. She couldn't take the failure in Mom's face, though. So, legs wobbling, she reclaims her spot in line.

Inner-she shrieks at her to get out because she's used to disappointing Mom.

Khalil ignores all social distancing protocols. He sidles up beside Trinity, bandana hanging around his neck. Trinity turns her attention to her iPhone.

"Why you at the Kroger's?" he asks. "You already

eat everything at home?"

"Go away, Khalil." Her voice breaks, so Khalil imitates her in a mocking tone.

She moves two spaces up in line as they open. Khalil follows. She tries sharing eye contact with the lady letting in people, maybe she could get Khalil to leave her alone. The lady is too busy or doesn't care. Trinity turns her back to her tormentor and pretends to play a game on her phone. Her hands tremble.

Inner-she is an electricity coursing through her, searching for escape.

"What's that, Infinity?"

"It's a phone, idiot."

Without warning, Khalil slaps Trinity across the wrist hard enough so the phone skitters from her hands. The sound when it hits the concrete is heartbreaking. "Now it's a broken phone. Idiot." He walks to the back of the line, cackling. His mother's Tesla is in a handicapped space, and laughing emerges from it, as well. The golden retriever puppy yaps incessantly.

Trinity scrambles for her continuation gift. The face is cracked. She hyperventilates. The security screen won't open, and out of panic, she pulls down her mask. The facial recognition works, and while its surface looks like a broken mirror, the apps do, too.

Two more spots open, and Trinity steps forward and pulls the mask back into place. She controls her breath and beats back the tears Khalil would love seeing.

Inner-she swims in virtual, violent, comforting scenarios to humiliate that jerk.

She hits the photos icon. The cracked material cuts her finger. While wiping the blood away with her Saint Motel tee-shirt, she must've hit the slideshow function. But something isn't right. The hope that the phone wasn't broke evaporates.

"Hey, pudgy," the lady behind her says. "It's your turn." A few more jeers arise from the crowd.

Trinity's legs move forward as if they belong to someone else, knees like rubber, ankles gelatinous. Inside the store, the florescent light wakes her from her trance. She looks around, sure everybody is staring at her and keeps moving to avoid being a sitting target. She finds the restroom. It's empty. Trinity locks the far stall door. Exhales. Opens the photo of Lara from school.

Inner-she dissolves a bit.

The photo of Lara making a smoochy face with the bunny-ears filter fades, but not completely. The outline remains, but another picture of Lara, one she'd never taken and in sepia tones, replaces it. This time Lara's in her bedroom, lit by candles. Her ever-present long sleeve is rolled up. A pattern of thin crosses covers her forearm, one bleeding. In her other hand, she holds a razor blade.

Inner-she can't recall Lara ever wearing short sleeves.

The photo dissolves into another color picture: Chloe from piano class, hugging her cat. Like Lara's photo, the shadow remains as it morphs. The sepia version shows Chloe slumping in her closet. An empty schnapps bottle lies on its side next to her.

Inner-she remembers how Mom and Chloe's grandmother always spoke in whispers. How they always found an excuse for Chloe to not spend the night.

The next picture is of her crush, Hadden, eating ice cream with whipped cream on his nose. Trinity's heart hastens as the sepia photo develops. It displays Hadden's hairless chest, a cigar being held to it by a large hairy hand. Several other circular marks scar his torso.

Inner-she's heart breaks with Trinity's.

The spell breaks when the restroom door opens. Trinity nearly drops her phone again. She finally inhales, not realizing she has held her breath. Once the other stall door closes, she exits. She can't focus, can't compute what the photos meant, if anything.

At the candy aisle, she stops, unable to take another step. Unaware of her, Khalil shoves handfuls of Almond Joys down his shorts. Trinity's arms shake so violently, she's afraid the camera won't focus. Three quick presses of the photo button, and she stumbles off to the soda aisle.

A lump in her throat proves too big to swallow. The blood rushes through her ears, audible, like a bad drummer. When the sepia picture of Khalil appears, Trinity yelps. "Dear, god, no." She knew he was a monster but couldn't imagine this.

Forgetting the cookie ingredients, she speed walks out of the store, bumping into the floral display at the entrance. When she sees the puppy in the Tesla, still yapping, seeming to smile, she almost loses it. She runs for the bus stop.

Inner-she boils with fury, her cries echoing through Trinity's soul.

———

In the locked bathroom at home, she practices what to say while she waits for the answer to her FaceTime call. A diplomatic way to ask doesn't find her consciousness. She reaches for the hang-up icon, but before she hits it, Lara appears.

"Hey, bruh." Lara's in her bedroom, surrounded by candles. Thick eyeliner circles her eyes. "How it's hanging?"

"Hola, bae." Trinity's voice trembled, but she put on her best face. "You surviving lockdown?"

"Only killed one of the parents. She was delicious."

Trinity forces a chuckle, but it's weak. The silence grows uncomfortable.

"You just call to see my pretty face?" Lara asks.

"That always makes my day. But I really just wanted to make sure you're okay."

"Why wouldn't I be okay? I mean, I've finished YouTube and am bored like in Ms. Matthew's science class, but I figure everybody is like that."

Another silence as Trinity gains courage. "We're friends, right?"

"Bruh, seriously? If you have to ask, maybe we ain't."

"If something was wrong, you'd tell me, right?" Trinity can't help it. Her eyes water.

"You're acting weird—even for you. What do you want?"

"Okay, this is gonna' sound cray, but," Trinity blew breath a long breath through her lips, "can I...well, can you show me your arm?"

"What?"

"I know. It's stupid"

"Why you wanna see my arm?"

"It's hard to explain—"

Lara shakes her head and purses her lips. "This is uber weird, bruh."

"I know, but please."

"Screw you, Trinity."

The screen darkens. Anxiety level seven hits.

Inner-she repeats how stupid of an idea this was.

The sepia tone appears again. Trinity sees Lara crying. Her sleeve exposes the cuts. She uses a razor blade to add another.

Trinity understands what she must do.

Inner-she confirms Trinity's instinct.

—

She sneaked out of the house before sunrise. Since both

Mom and Dad work from home now, they tend to sleep in. Trinity plans to be back before they awaken.

Sitting on the sidewalk outside the white plastic fence on Azul Ave, she waits. It's on the nice side of Negro Arroyo Blvd—the side north of Rouge. The sidewalk is hard and warm, and as early as it is, Trinity knows the day is going to be filled with sweat and heat rashes. She fights the urge to leave. To return home and put Khalil and his bullying in the past.

Inner-she stops her every time, reminding Trinity of the disgusting images her cracked iPhone stores inside.

Finally, the back door slides open. The familiar, vulgar voice yells, "Get out, stupid. Quit pooping on the floor." A few seconds slip past. "GO!" A yelp pierces the air.

Inner-she erupts in anger.

Trinity's heart quickens. Anxiety level ten achieved. She's nearly paralyzed and can't keep up with the thousands of thoughts crashing in her head.

The glass sliding door slams shut.

Inner-she tells Trinity it's time.

She checks up and down Azul, confirming nobody watches her. Keeping her back against the warm fence, she slides around the corner. Trinity's Chuck Taylors catch the edging and she stumbles into the rock landscape. In her mind, it sounds like an explosion, and she freezes. The puppy yips, but nobody else comes out to investigate.

Straightening up, Trinity makes her way to the gate. She unhooks the latch, the click loud as a gunshot.

The back yard is a field of weeds and bare dirt. The puppy shakes and cowers. Trinity removes the beef jerky from her sweats pocket.

"C'mere, baby," she whispers.

The golden retriever answers with a whimper. It's a good fifteen yards away. Trinity makes kissing sounds and offers a piece of the jerky.

Inner-she calls for the dog, willing it forward.

It doesn't help. The puppy sits, front two legs walking in place, head bobbing and tail wagging at its tip. But it doesn't come forward.

Walking in a crouch, Trinity enters the back yard. Her nerves hum. She wags the jerky. "C'mon, pup." Trinity glances at the door, checking for her nemesis. She takes another step forward and tosses the dried meat chunk. It lands fifteen feet away from its target.

Inner-she mocks Trinity for her lack of athleticism, but apologizes quickly.

The puppy slides forward. When it raises to all fours, it limps. The dog's head remains cowed, but it approaches the offering with caution. Once it reaches the jerky, it allows a perfunctory sniff before guzzling down the treat. The tail wag goes turbo. It yelps again.

Trinity allows another glance at the house. Inches forward. Offers another piece.

The puppy limps closer, something off with its right hind leg. It whimpers with each step. The closer it gets, the quicker its pace.

Trinity's impatience gets the best of her, and she sprints forth, gathers the pup and heads for stage left exit. But while shifting the dog's weight, she hits a sore spot and the retriever releases a yelp that could be heard on Venus. As they clear the gate, the sliding door opens.

Stumbling down the sidewalk, each step keeping her from falling as much as it's propelling her forward, she hears the horrible voice behind her, "Come back here!"

Inner-she tells Trinity not to go back.

Inner-she says she's got this one.

—

Trinity's mind's a fog when she wakes up. It takes some time before she concludes she's in her room. Still, she's unsure of how much she dreamed if any of the gruesome images she endured actually existed. Her sane brain says none of it, but whose sane brain works properly?

She pulls the Princes Leia blanket off. Her sheets are and sweats are soaked with blood. Trinity begins a scream that stops in her throat.

Inner-she tells her to calm down.

Her mind dances in space for a long time. Until the puppy licks her face. Trinity remembers everything.

Inner-she smiles. Says goodbye.

They decide to name the dog Hadden.

High school will be fine.

THE GIRL FROM THE END OF THE BAR

That's her, all right. Oh, that's her.

No doubt. Even without my specs that she broke, I can tell. With that black hair. With that tight, white, just-right hootchie dress that's an inch from a show-you-my-cootchie dress. With that ass. With that ass. With *that* ass.

That's her, all right. The girl who talked to herself—to her twin, she said, though no twin joined us at the bar. Oh, that's fuckin' her.

In the yellow light of the long hall, the light bouncing off yellow walls and the light the geometrical-patterned carpet sucks dead, in that yellow light, from this distance, she looks smaller. Weaker. She looks scared. With that fucking ass she looks fucking scared.

That's her, all right. Still talking to herself, but too far away for me to eavesdrop.

The carpet tips the hall, and she seems a mile and a day away. With each of my steps, she escapes another mile. The hall's yellow walls with its hordes of intermittent doors keep me erect. Not in that way. Not with that white dress and that white ass. I'm erect that right way already, all right? The walls, yellow and all, catch me, bounce me back across the interlocking puked-on puzzle pieces constructing the carpet, over to the other yellow wall that bounces me back yet again.

I wave. "Hold up. Stop," I say. I slur—let's face it, I slur. "Hold up."

She doesn't wave. She just frets and fiddles and fucks with the door.

And I shouldn't—I truly shouldn't—but I'm drunk and don't give a donkey fuck, and it hurts when she doesn't return my generous gesture. I deserve at least a wave. I deserve that. At least a nod. After everything tonight? I deserve that.

Still her and her ass, her fucking fuckable ass, don't wave, don't nod. They, her and her ass, release a squeal that's not pleasant. Not a scream, a squeal, like one of them sorry whores in one of them sorry movies, waiting for a sorry excuse for a villain to kill them. That squeal.

"Go away." She says it to me, not to the twin who's not there. "I'm warning you."

So, right then, I realize I'm Jason or Freddie or Michael Myers or Jack Torrance. Or Stan. Because if I'd star in one of those movies, somehow they'd name me: Stan. That's a solid character name right there.

"He's still coming," she says, and it's not to me. "I warned him."

I'll admit, the twin thing, that's a little creepy. Not that she has one, if she does, but the talking to herself? What's with that?

Confession time: At the bar, I might have possibly,

plausibly, probably told her I was left-handed and explained it's likely, logically because I ate my twin in the womb. Possibly. When she looked at me like I had a third eye, I had to explain the theory that all left handed people were once twins. Not that I believe it, but it's out there. Fetal resorption—it's a thing.

I look to my feet, assuring I can take the next step. Don't know if I can, but do anyway. My heel finds firm ground on the octagon or pentagon or pentagram or octagram that fits into the next carpet tile, and the wall bounces me up. Fuck, didn't seem like I drank much. Not near as much as she did, but it's hit me full-face-full-fucking on. Must be the altitude. Must be. Has to be.

"Hey, smile for me," I say. I slur. "Hey, it's me, man. It's me."

I wave again. She doesn't. Again.

The mile away she was is now a half mile in the hallway from hell with the tipped, trippy carpet, and it's her. It's her, all right. With that ass and that dress and the sixty bucks of damn drinks in her she'd made me buy.

Can't she spare at least a wave? A fucking wave? I'm not asking for a blow job here. I'm not a rapist. Yet. I mean, that's a joke, but, seriously. Wouldn't a reasonably priced hooker let me tickle her tonsils for sixty dollars? I'm not asking that from her in the white dress with the white ass and the white knuckles that can't fit her card in the door's reader. I'm not. But a nod? A wave? An acknowledgement that I chose to spend my money on her, my time with her, at that seedy-ass, horrible hotel bar rather than finish my novel (fucking novel) in my room or invest that hard-earned money and hard-earned hard-on in a sixty-dollar heavenly hummer. And not even a wave?

She doesn't.

She's scared. She's trying not to show it, but her and I know it—she's fucking scared, and I want to laugh. It's not like I'm a rapist or anything. I'm not.

Yet.

And I shouldn't—I really shouldn't—but I do. I duck my head, furrow my brow, inflate my chest, growl grotesquely. I shouldn't, but I do and it's funnier than it sounds. I'm already scary sweaty from the old hotel's old radiators—a man, my size, my age, doesn't sweat. We render. I say, "You didn't think it would be that easy, did you?" I slur. I mean, for sixty bucks, for a fucking forfeited tangy tongue massage, I should have some fun. Who could begrudge that? Sixty bucks is sixty bucks, and I won't hurt her. I'm not a rapist.

"Leave me alone!"

"But I'm not a rapist." Yet. "It's me. From the end of the bar. I thought we were cool."

"I just met you," she says. She doesn't slur like me.

"And this is crazy?" And it is. Why couldn't she just have waved? Why she got to be so hideously hostile? I mean, sixty bucks. It isn't a lot, but, I'm like invested here now.

It has to be the altitude. Or maybe I should have eaten more for dinner than a half bag of Diablo Doritos and convenience-store sushi. Maybe, it's simply convenience-store sushi, but I'm mucho mucho more drunk than I should be. It's only been six months sobriety I threw away tonight. This pussy of a lightweight after six months? Doesn't compute, but I have to be furiously fucked-up to possess the inkling to think these thoughts I'm thinking.

They're there, though.

Although, if I were to let go, allow my novel's characters to take over just this one time, the one time where I can claim to be too drunk to remember or act responsibly, too passionate to pretend coherence, this—right now—would be the chance. And the wife has been on me to take more chances.

That's why I'm here anyway, right? At this creepy mountain hotel to finish the last chapter of the last novel (fucking novel), and what better way than to live its lasciviousness from my character's head and all its nothingness. Here, away from the wife whom I love but can't stand. Away from the agent. In the hotel where nobody knows anybody's name? Nobody knows where I'm at or who I really am. Not her. Not her. Definitely not her.

And I'll be gone by morning. Bitch should have waved.

"Why'd you break my glasses, man?" It's a responsible, reasonable remark. I wave still.

"Because you wouldn't stop staring."

She has that righteously right. With that black hair and those bomb breasts and that tight-white, just-right delightfully delectable dress.

Nobody knows I'm here. I'm registered under a different name. If it were ever to happen and, you know, somebody could get away with it some sick night, tonight is that night. And she's scared, but she hides it so well. Too well, and it kind of irks me.

"I thought we were cool," I slur. I say.

The half-mile has shrunk to a quarter. The shapes on the floor shift and shimmer and sparkle and spin. The octogram becomes a pentagram onto which I step before it lurches me forward to an octagon. Hotel carpets are a trip, man.

"Please. I have to help my sister. She's missed her medicine. Go back to the bar." Her voice doesn't sound urgent, though. In my novel, the one that won't finish itself (fucking novel), its ending anyway, this seems just the thing. "Stay away! I'm not warning you again."

Her pouty lips are the perfect playground for some oral origami. Say sixty bucks worth? That's what my character, Stan, would figure, anyway. There's nothing wrong thinking about it. I won't do anything, but it's kind of fun to imagine. I mean, who hasn't thought of pulling a fire alarm to get out of a test at school or a meeting at work? People don't do those things, but they think about them. Stan thinks about them. It's okay to think about them. I'm a writer, after all. I'm supposed to consciously conjure up this crap. I have to go to dark places, man. Some seriously dark places.

"Your sister?" I ask. "The twin's in there?" I can't help but think it: wouldn't that mean just thirty dollars apiece? What a bargain. But I'd never do that. Stan? Stan would terrorize and traumatize the twins with fury and a flurry of fantastical fetishes, and leave them fucking huddled together, crying in the corner. Before he killed them. That's Stan though.

I'm not Stan. Yet.

She jams the keycard against the door, missing the slot by several inches. As the quarter mile distance closes to a tenth, I see her better, although still fuzzy without my specs. I see she's not got the keycard anywhere close to the slot. I see she might not be scared at all. I deserve her to be a little afraid, right? I mean all those drinks and all my imagined menace.

No nod. No wave. Now, no scare?

This feels more like a challenge rather than the distraction from the novel (fucking novel) I intended when I finally succumbed to the beckoning bar. Enough with Stan, the character, and his stupid problems, I thought. One drink would calm my meandering mind. One teensy-weensy drink, and who would know? Not my wife, like she didn't expect me to anyway. Not my agent who gave up on me years ago. One drink, but there she was in that tight, white dress. Mumbling to her twin.

"Who's gonna pay for my glasses? I can't drive

without them," I slur. I lie.

"You were looking at me funny. Like I disgusted you," she says.

"I did?" And I guess I did when the booze kicked full-on full in. For a moment, my vision blurred. My mind, as it does, went to one of those dark places and she wasn't the gorgeous girl with that white ass. But my mind does that in its writerly way.

"Fine," I say, because dialogue's never been my strong point. "Ask me in for a night cap, and we'll call it even."

"I think you'd regret it if I did."

"Try me." I lean against my arm against the wall, trying on my macho smooth pose, but mostly to keep from falling. I picture the felonious fellatio from her and her sister waiting behind the door to room 217.

"This is your chance." I've never heard the voice before, but know it immediately. "Sure, you might regret it, but probably not as much as you'd regret missing it. Chances don't come along like this." And Stan makes a surprising amount of sense somehow.

"Will he do?" She's not talking to me. "You need your medicine."

"Think about it, man. Two for one, and tomorrow you're gone. No witnesses, nobody looking for you. Just their vague idea of you." If it weren't for the erection thrusting against my zipper, maybe it wouldn't make such sensational sense. But after the drinks and her attitude and the no wave/no nod policy she's shown, it doesn't sound so creepy and crazy. It'd be research, for the novel. To blow the agent away who said I write with no verisimilitude. I do this, I'd have verisimilitude out my ass!

"So, we gonna do this or what?" she says, but I'm not sure if she's talking to me.

"Couldn't stop now even if I tried."

"Most honest thing you said all night." The keycard finds the slot on the first shot and the door flies open as I gaze at the gap in her space, with the nylons stretched to waste and her thick, thick, thick thighs.

The door opens further than she intends. In the dark, I catch a shadow, but without my specs, it's more a blur. "Would you like to come in?"

And I shouldn't—I really shouldn't—but want to so fucking bad.

"We're going to crush that pretty little throat in our hands, and she's going to look you in the eye and think she should've been nicer." As drunk as I am, as out-of-my-mind horny as I am, it doesn't sound so outrageous.

"Pretend she's my wife, that horrible bitch you gave me in your kind-of-horrible novel. Pretend her and the twin deserve it as much as that twat. Cutting me off, making me feel like I'm unworthy of her. Nagging every time I sneak a little nip to take the edge off. Isn't that how this bitch in the white dress with the white ass made you feel?"

Stan is tough to argue with when he's right all the

time. I wish he would assert himself in the novel a little more. Bastard.

"The other one, the twin who has to look at least this good, imagine she's your agent who ain't sold your shit in years." Based upon the shadow I saw, she's not. "You hear that, my man? That's opportunity knocking, Sparky." I imagine the vertebrae cracking in my hands, her eyes bulging from her head, her blood flowing down my forearms. I'm harder than Chinese arithmetic. I think for the first time, I might be, I am, going through with this.

"Go get that fanciful facial fuck, and stick a pinky up her ass. For sixty bucks, pinkie penetration should be expected." Who can argue with such logic? It's as obvious as the bulge in my khakis.

So, in my writerly mind, I cross the line and decide I'll be a rapist and a killer. It's time, and I'll worry about everything else tomorrow. A small part of me is ashamed at how easy I caved, but I clear away that polluted convoluted thought. Tomorrow, it'll be fine.

Still, even in my way-too-inebriated state, I can't push away what I've just seen behind the door, when it was opened too much by the whore. Inside, before she in the white dress with the white ass grabbed the knob and closed the view, I think I saw what I'd seen before she'd broke my glasses.

"Focus, my friend. If not now, when?"

"Well," she says, "you want in or not?"

"Like nothing else I've ever wanted." I say, blinded

by visions of painting the room with her blood. You know, for the book. Verisimilitude, motherfuckers.

Then, my writerly mind goes there, and I see my wife. I see her crying, which I could never take. What kind of monster makes his wife cry? Reality punches me between the eyes and my erection dies, shrinks to half its size.

For a second, though, a long, long second, I thought I'd do it, but who am I kidding? I kill people on the page—apparently without verisimilitude. I need to get back to it and get the fuck out of this hotel. It's messed with my head enough.

I step toward her, planning to peck her on the cheek and bid her and her bod and the white dress a fine adieu, maybe whisper in her ear how lucky she is to get away, but without the walls willing assistance, my knee buckles like a tiny twig. She, in her white dress with that white ass, catches me as if she expected my demise.

She smirks. "For such a big fella, you don't handle your liquor so well." A little laugh lisps past her lips. "You're kind of a pussy, huh? The big bad man have too much for his little heart?"

"I'm sorry," I say, I slur. "I should be heading..."

She hooks her hands together around my chest, weaves her arms beneath my armpits. She's stronger than she looks and drags me inside as if I'm on oversized ragdoll. Across the trippy hall carpet, my heels leave a tattered trail.

"Dude, you're fucked." I'd tell Stan thank you, but I'm too terrified to operate my mouth. My writerly mind, though, it works fine and dashes in a billion different directions—all of them awful.

The room has to be a hundred degrees and smells like a fat girl's flatulent ass on a sweltering summer Sunday. I kick as much as my body allows, which is pathetic. The girl with the tight-white, just right hootchie dress that's an inch from a show-you-my cootchie dress drops me on the sticky, damp carpet. "This is it for this spot," she says, but not to me. To the shadow. "We got to make tracks, post haste."

Just as my eyes start adjusting to the dark, the lights flash on. I'm flat on my stomach. Nose hovering inches from a dark stain covering the carpet. The girl in the white dress kicks me over so I can see the beast on the king-sized bed. The one I glanced outside the door but chose to ignore because Stan urged me on, before he was gone. She's at least three-hundred pounds, naked and so translucent, her green veins look like tattoos beneath her skin. Against her enormous, cellulite scarred breasts, she holds what appears to be a baby. The ugliest, unluckiest baby ever born.

I scream, but it's weak. I see the baby isn't separate from the beast at all, but a growth from her abdomen.

"Still want that night cap?" she asks. One of them asks. Without my specs, I can't quite tell, but I swear it's the growth.

Again, I can't respond.

"Jesus Christ!" the beast says. "How much of that shit did you give him?"

The bitch Cosby-ed me, and I'm too weak to tell her how pissed I am. I wish I would have killed her now.

"I can't take him now," says the beast, and I think that's terribly nice of her. "Not when he's that fucked up. You want to kill Trinity?" The beast pets the baby's misshapen head.

The girl with the white dress takes it off and begins feeding from the other breast of the doughy woman. She rests between gulps, but won't look at me.

From the bed, the feeder says, "Don't worry, nobody knows he's here. It's perfect."

I shouldn't—I really shouldn't—but I cry without the ability to cry. My mind quits, even though my body's beaten it to that conclusion.

"I know," the other one says. "I just hate watching you take your medicine."

YAKUZA PRINCESS

The Monday she'd find her business partner sawn clean in half, Katsumi Tanaka arrived late at the office. Up most the night waiting for a message from Devon, the rest spent worrying about her scheduled surgery, sleep had teased her until sunrise.

Wrecked, half delusional and full pissed off, she pulled in just after eleven and promptly spilled her Duncan Donuts coffee, cementing her excellent start to the day. She parked outside their warehouse beside Devon's Corvette occupying its predetermined space under the Tanaka and Lombardo's Imports sign. They shared the warehouse with two cannabis grow houses and a chop shop where everybody spoke anything but English. The end unit with no signage was occupied by super shady characters the other tenets had silently agreed not to discuss.

Katsumi called Devon again. Again, the call forwarded straight to voicemail. Curses in both English and Japanese flowed freely from her.

She cut the Hummer's engine, killing the Hamilton soundtrack mid-rhyme, and searched her enormous purse for the Robocop Auto-9. Its handle had been specially modified to fit her missing pinkie. Her trigger finger felt itchy. Her gut told her to run. Her code overruled that instinct.

Inside, Mitzi's receptionist desk sat abandoned, a

sign of how bad things actually were. The phone rang—unanswered. The desk chair had been tipped over, and the kitten poster displaying the 'Hang in there, it's almost Friday' motto had been torn, the bottom third missing.

Katsumi removed her heels. She smelled the air for danger, and it reeked of death.

Devon Lombardo's door—complete with a nameplate stating 'What, me worry?'—stood ajar. Silence swallowed his office.

Back pressed against the reception area's faux-wood paneling, Katsumi tried glimpsing anything inside. After an eon or so, she nudged the door open with the Robocop's barrel. Before she caught a decent peek, a hand grasped her wrist, dug in fingernails so Katsumi bled, and yanked her into the maw.

The automatic fired two rounds as Katsumi somersaulted over the blood-coated floor. Old instincts took over. She landed on her bare feet, pistol aimed at her attacker. A tenth of a nanosecond before she fired, Katsumi removed her finger from the trigger and trembled at thoughts of what she might've done. Breath flooded her lungs. Thick fluid gushed between her toes. The Robocop Auto-9 splashed in the red pond beneath their feet.

"Konnichiwa, papa-san." The young woman pulled a viscera-covered wire taught with both hands. "Or do I not call you that anymore?" she said in Japanese.

Sticky blood from the floor drenched Katsumi's

white pantsuit. She noted the carnage in her peripheral vision but could only focus on the woman.

The daughter she'd abandoned fifty-five hundred miles away and almost a half-decade ago.

"Miyu?"

—

Four years earlier:

Akira Tanaka melted in the steam of the mushiburo, embarrassed by his fraud of a body. The serpent tattoos covering his back and torso couldn't hide his shame, and his skin belonged as much to his irizume artist as it did to himself.

Beside him, Yoshi Ito sat naked except for the shoulder holster complete with pistol. Sweat ran in rivulets through the creases of his fat. His arrogance stank nearly as bad as he. Ito wasn't just a cop. He headed the narcotics division in Tokyo's Ginza District. Ito's team focused on the new Yakuza that'd abandoned the ancient Bushido principals. The Yakuza Akira worked for as a waka gashira, an officer one step below the boss or oyabun.

Ito passed the mirror, cleaned the stray powder from his nose, and guided the bobbing head of the young girl working his cock. She must've gotten paid by the decibel because she sucked like a wet-vac on its last legs.

Akira rested the mirror on the girl's bare ass and killed the remaining two lines in efficient fashion. He snorted like a horse afterward, wiping the trickle of blood from his moustache.

"Things," Ito said mid-orgasm, "they're not like when the Yakuza had honor, you understand?"

The mirror tumbled from the girl's posterior and broke across the sauna's wooden floor. She gagged on the cop's cum but choked it down. Ito slapped her across the face anyway.

The girl collapsed into the broken glass. Ito palmed her head, ponytail threaded between his index and middle finger, and ground her face into the shards. "That was my wife's mirror!" A dark red pool stained the planks. The girl yelped, gurgled inhuman sounds, and begged forgiveness. Ito mashed with more vigor. He cackled in cartoonish syllables that shook the sauna.

When he eventually released the prostitute, she lay face down for an uneasy length of time. Akira's heart thundered from cocaine and fear. Despite the decades of violence he'd witnessed and dealt out, his stomach churned at seeing a woman on the wrong end of it.

The girl rolled over at last, babbling. Her mangled nose hung by a slice of skin. Cuts ravaged her cheeks. She coughed and spat a tooth free.

Ito guffawed. "I hope you're good with puzzles. Your face might be missing some pieces." Reaching into his robe hung from the door, he removed a sizeable wad of yen. He threw the bills at her. "Be gone, sow," he said in English, but mocked it by delivering a Godzilla pantomime with poor dubbing and overt gesticulation.

The girl writhed on the floor. Mirror fragments dug into her.

"We have business, Akira-san." Ito wiped sweat from his eye. "You're not going to be happy," he said in Japanese.

Akira braced for the shakedown. "Suzuki-sama will not be pleased. Your expense is cutting deeply into the clan's profits. We cannot pay more."

As the girl pushed herself into a sitting posture, Ito stared at her and avoided Akira's glare. "Don't be silly. Based on what I'm seeing, you're profiting too much."

"There is no such thing." Akira freed a cigarette pack from his robe pocket and offered one to the cop. He lit Ito's first.

"There is when the media reports it. Drug crimes are up. It's making the police look bad."

"Because you're arresting people?"

"Because we have to."

The girl finally found her feet. She removed a shard from her thigh. Akira thought she'd gotten a head start on the seven years of bad luck.

"How much are you asking for, you parasite?"

"Money will not solve this."

Holding the piece of mirror up to inspect her face, the girl screamed. Not in pain, but in horror. She launched for the cop.

Without blinking, Ito slipped free his pistol and fired. He hit her in mid jump. The shot took half her head off. Her mutilated nose landed in Akira's lap, and her body dropped to the floor with a splat.

The sauna door flung open and a uniformed officer entered. Upon seeing the dead mass of hooker, the blood ran from his face. Confusion glazed his features.

Ito lifted his hand in a stop signal and nodded. "Wait in the car. I'll call you when we're finished."

After a moment spent gathering himself, the young cop bowed. He shakily exited and closed the door.

Akira picked the nose from his thighs, inspected it for a moment before flicking it atop the dead woman. He wore nonchalance, but his thoughts ran at a million kilometers a second.

Ito inhaled off his cigarette and blew a train of smoke rings as if the fifty kilograms of dead twenty-year old didn't bleed out a meter away from his feet. "Money will not quiet the media. They're calling for action."

Closing his eyes and catching his breath, Akira calmed the tremors begging for escape from inside him. He focused on the conversation. "What are you calling for? That's my only concern."

"A sacrifice." The cop cracked a half smile and turned to look Akira in the eye.

"Oh, that's all." Akira pointed to the corpse. "I think you have one."

"No, Akira-san. I need one that I can put in the news reports."

Akira took a drag and blew the smoke plume out the side of his mouth. "You're getting cryptic in your old age."

"Apologies. I guess one tries to dance around bad news." Ito rubbed his cigarette out on the bench and tossed the remaining three-quarters of it into the lava-rock pit situated in the center of the room. "The public is clamoring for an arrest. Not of some child from the clan, but a bigger fish. My department is pressuring me to pacify the media's outrage."

"How big of a fish?"

"Not as large as an oyabun."

Akira held his hands up to show length. He started with them a few centimeters from each other. Ito shook his head. Akira spread his hands farther apart. Ito continued shaking "no."

"Maybe waka gashira size?"

Ito picked the pistol up from the bench and pointed it at Akira. "Exactly waka gashira sized."

"I think you run the risk of upsetting Suzuki-sama by arresting his number two."

"Not according to oyobun Suzuki."

Air evacuated Akira's chest. With Japan's strict drug laws he could be put away for decades. Especially considering it would be a show trial. His family would be disgraced.

"I trust you to be a man of honor and accept your fate." Ito stood and waved the gun as a signal that Akira should join him.

Akira raised his arms, stopping mid gesture to hit his cigarette, and stood.

"Get your clothes on."

Akira then realized Ito would watch him dress. The thought urged him to action. He threw both hands down, catching Ito on the wrist. The gun slid from the cop's sweaty hand and clattered against the floor planks. Before Ito could react, Akira drove a knee into his crotch.

Ito dropped to his knees, landing on a mirror shard. Akira pounced. He threw his opponent into a headlock and put his cigarette out on the fat man's sweaty forehead. As the odor of burnt flesh wafted, Ito screamed at a higher pitch than the dead prostitute had.

Grabbing the cop by his shoulder holster, Akira lifted him up and ran him head-first into the raised lava-rock pit, stepping on the corpse in the process. The ribcage gave way and her chest swallowed his foot. He felt the guts ooze between his toes as he dragged her forth. Adrenaline wouldn't allow for such a distraction, though. Akira pulled the half-conscious cop up by his hair. The man flailed and swung but connected with nothing but air.

Akira guided Ito's head to the lava rocks. The hissing of his flesh competed with Ito's shrieks. He spasmed wildly, but Akira put his full weight into the back of the cop's head. The sauna smelled like a kitchen cooking pork.

On the pit's tiled ledge rested a ceramic urn of water used to create the mushiburo's steam. Akira grabbed the vessel and poured its contents over the back of Ito's head. A cloud of steam billowed, and the water boiled upon contact with the heated rocks. A few seconds later, Ito quit fighting.

Kicking free of the girl's body, a stretch of intestine snagged Akira's foot. He had to lean over and pull it out from between his toes. The gun lay on the wooden floor, and Akira took it with him.

He scrambled for the dressing room. There, he slid on his satin panties and garter belt, then pulled up his suit paints. He left his shirt unbuttoned and nabbed the jacket from its hanger before escaping out the alley door. His brassiere remained behind in the locker.

—

Back at the warehouse:

The upper half of Devon Lombardo's body lay splayed atop his cocobolo desk. Blood still dripped onto the concrete floor, making tiny splashes in the collected pool. Katsumi could see one foot peeking out behind the desk. The Gucci loafer had been dyed red.

The receptionist, Mitzi, hung from a wire noose secured around an iron I-beam rafter. Her tongue lulled out the side of her mouth. Crimson covered her orthopedic stockings and a shoe had fallen from her left foot.

"America, papa-san?" Miyu shook her head in disappointment. "You abandon me and mother for this shithole, America?"

"What are you doing here?" Katsumi asked in

Japanese.

Miyu nodded to the dead bodies. "I'm killing motherfuckers."

The shock of seeing her girl all grown merged with the jolt of finding her partner and receptionist murdered. It kept Katsumi's thoughts from connecting. She didn't know if she should hug the girl or run. So she just gazed.

Miyu could have passed for her mother from twenty years earlier. Except for the Yakuza irizume desecrating her arms. The way her yellow tank top was draped allowed Katsumi to see that the tattoos likely covered her daughter's back and torso, as well. All serpents and cherry blossoms. Of course, cherry blossoms.

"Has the clan sunk low enough they need to recruit women now?"

A fire flared from Miyu's eyes. She inherited that expression from her mother, too. "Suzuki-sama is the only family I have left. And I'm a far better Yakuza than you ever hoped to be." She pulled the piano wire she held tight and in a threatening manner.

"I'm so proud." Katsumi bent and retrieved her Robocop Auto-9. She wiped it off on an unsoiled portion of her jumpsuit. Then it hit her. "Wait. What happened to your mother?"

Miyu laughed like a child had asked her a silly question. "You think she could survive the dishonor? We were shunned and broke, and our names were wedded to a Yakuza drug runner. You brought shame to the Tanaka name and the Suzuki clan, then slithered away like a snake in the night."

Katsumi barely heard the latter part of the diatribe. The news nearly knocked her over as a million pounds of guilt landed on her shoulders. "I had no choice."

"Bullshit! You could've taken us with you. You could've not lied to me."

While Miyu spoke the truth, Katsumi also had. She'd never fulfill who she truly was if she remained in that family. Her escape was from everything—the police, the Yakuza, her former body. The price was her family. Very steep, but in her final estimation, fair.

"So Suzuki is how you found me?" she said to change the subject.

"It wasn't as easy as that, but after what you did to Yoshi Ito, there were a lot of people interested in tracking you down." Miyo wound and unwound the piano wire. "We had a lot of help. And you vanishing with two-billion yen made things a little easier."

"I'm sorry for killing Ito-san," she lied. "It haunts my every breath."

"Oh, that motherfucker isn't dead." Miyu began pacing in slow steps. "You're lucky I found you before him."

Hearing Ito had survived shook her to the core, but Katsumi needed to remain single-minded. "And now that you found me, what?"

"I have a job to do."

156 / SAM W. ANDERSON

"What? You'd kill your own father? For your oyabun?"

"I'd kill Emperor Naruhito himself for Suzuki-sama." Her pacing hastened. "That's the code of the Yakuza."

—

The Tanaka apartment in Tokyo, four years earlier:
Miyu awoke in the middle of the night to rustling outside her sleeping chamber. From beneath the door, she saw shadows. Grunts and heavy breathing filled the hallway. Not again, she thought.

Springing from tatami mat, she grabbed her robe and exited the room. "Where are you going?" Her voice was a loud whisper.

Her father stood by the front door. Stacked beside him, four large canvas knapsacks teetered. "I have a work errand to run."

"Now?" Miyu tiptoed over the cold tile floor.

"You know my job, Cherry Blossom. They call, I come."

Miyu didn't really know his job—only suspected. The subject was forbidden from discussion, but the snide remarks from fellow prep-school students kind of confirmed her hunches. "Will you be back in time to go to the driving range? You promised."

"Yes. The driving range, then sushi."

"And you'll let me have sake?"

"Miyu-chan. Don't push it."

Miyu tied her robe's obi and pointed to her father's

shirttail. "Your shirt's buttoned wrong."

He looked down and chuckled. "Thanks."

"These bags for work?" she tried lifting the top one by the strap, but it was too heavy from her angle.

"Leave those alone." Her father finished re-doing his buttons. He leaned and kissed her on the head. "You get back to sleep. I have to go."

"Goodnight, papa-san." Miyu headed for her room, stepping quietly so as not to wake her mother.

"Miyu," her father called.

She stopped and turned.

"I love you, Cherry Blossom. You're a fine young lady."

After returning to her tatami, Miyu couldn't sleep. It took a while to comprehend why her father's words seemed so odd, but she realized he hadn't said them in years. Despair blanketed her, and she tossed and turned. After several more minutes, she heard the front door close.

She poked her head into the hallway, confirming her father had left. Jogging softly, she made her way to the kitchen. In the third cupboard, behind a family-size bag of rice, she found the box of chocolate Pocky and giggled to herself. As she made her getaway to her room, she came to an abrupt stop. Something wasn't right.

Miyu looked about. It took a half a minute before she noticed the family picture in the hall was missing.

She ran to her room and looked out the window at

the street. Her father's Lexus emerged from the parking garage. Something heavy obviously weighed the trunk down as the taillights disappeared around the corner.

Miyu swallowed hard and knelt. She cried quietly. Again, she didn't want to wake her mother.

—

Devon Lombardi's blood-splattered office:

"You still owe me sushi, motherfucker." Miyu stomped through the blood, her agitation growing more evident with each step.

"I gather you're not in the mood to grab some right now?"

Before her daughter could answer, a loud thump emerged from behind them and made Katsumi jump. She turned to see Mitzi's headless body soaking up blood from the floor. Katsumi looked to the rafters in time to see Mitzi's head slip from the wire noose. It splattered across the concrete. Her brain rolled free from the cracked skull and slid several feet over the blood and left a slimy wake.

"That's gonna be a bitch to clean," Katsumi said.

"At least you won't have to worry about it."

"Come now, Cherry Blossom. Wh--"

"You don't get to call me that, anymore!" Spittle flew from Miyu's lips as she yelled.

"I'm sorry. You're right. I left that privilege in Tokyo."

Miyu unwound the wire around her hands more

and yanked it taught again. Her strides grew longer. Red stains soaked the cuffs of her Levi's.

"Miyu? What are you going to do?" Katsumi held the gun up as if it spoke for itself.

"Suzuiki-sama and Ito-san demanded that I torture you and make you tell me where their money is." She unwound the wire more so she could extend her arms their full length. "They want you to spend your last hours in agony."

"Well, fuck them. I guess they didn't foresee me having a gun the size of your head, did they."

"I advise you quit threatening me, or I might take their wishes to heart."

Katsumi had had about enough. She pointed the gun at her daughter. "Drop the wire."

"Or what?"

She hadn't considered such a response.

Miyu stopped pacing. She broke into a smug smile. "You'd shoot your own daughter, papa-san?"

"A daughter that promised to torture me for hours? Let's just say, I'm not getting you any saki with your sushi."

Miyu spread her arms as if on a cross. "Take your shot."

A mass formed in Katsumi's gut. "Don't think I won't."

"That gun's as worthless to you as it is to me." Miyu took two steps forward, her smile growing. "You love me remember? I'm a fine young woman, aren't I? You said so yourself."

The possibility of Miyu calling his bluff until he could bluff no more entered Katsumi's mind. The heavy gun shook in her hand.

The girl moved closer. She pulled the piano wire so tight, it twanged.

Katsumi stepped back. Her foot slipped in the blood, but she caught herself before falling.

"Just so you know," Miyu said, "I don't need to torture you to find the money. I found all your papers in your desk while I was waiting for you. Bank statements. The sticky note with your laptop password." Miyu strode another stride forward. "The will."

The Robocop Auto-9 weighed a million pounds, and sweat covered Katsumi's palms making it more difficult to grip the weapon. "That's close enough. Put the fucking wire down before somebody gets dead."

"I should thank you for leaving everything to me. Doesn't make up for the shit you pulled, but it's a nice start."

"Not one more step, Miyu. I swear I'll shoot you right in the fucking head."

Miyu stepped forward again.

Katsumi paced back another step. "Don't make me do this."

Another stride by Miyu. "What are you waiting for, papa-san?"

Katsumi fired. The bullet sailed several feet over

her daughter's head. "You get one warning shot."

Again, Miyu drew closer.

"Goddamnit! Stop! Stop or I'll kill you."

"No, you won't."

The step back landed her foot atop Mitzi's brain. The organ squished between Katsumi's toes causing a flashback to the private sauna in Ginza and the dead hooker. Again, she'd had enough. Katsumi brought up her left hand to steady her aim.

Before Katsumi pulled the trigger, Miyu reached behind her head and flung an object toward Katsumi. As the knife drove through her skull, her mind registered what it was. She never got a second shot off.

—

Miyu walked quickly to the cargo van waiting outside the warehouse. She checked over both shoulders to see if anybody noticed her but saw nothing. Sticky fluid gushed in her Chuck Taylors as she strode. After taking a final look around, she opened the passenger-side door and got in.

Her hands trembled and she fought back the vomit fighting for escape.

"Is it done?" Ito asked. A large eye patch with the Japanese flag obscured half his malformed head. Black craters covered his face, and his lack of upper lip exposed crooked teeth and provided no break from his rotten breath.

Miyu nodded. "She's dead." She fiddled with the piano wire out of anxiety.

"Did he tell you how to get the money?"

"No."

"Did he suffer."

Miyu bit her lip and swallowed hard. "Physically? No. No, she didn't"

"What? I told Suzuki never to send a woman for man's work."

"I suggest we get out of here before somebody notices us."

When Ito checked the side mirror for traffic, Miyu reached over his head. She twisted the wire behind his neck.

He gurgled as the blood ran like a river from his trachea.

Miyu continued twisting and tightening the wire. It took a good five minutes before Ito's head lopped off, landing in his lap.

"You don't torture your father. That's Yakuza code."

Back inside the warehouse, before she grabbed the car keys from the dead Italian guy—she'd wanted a Corvette since she was a little girl—she entered her father's office for one last errand.

The picture on his desk remained in the same frame it had been in when it hung on the apartment's hallway wall. She tucked it under her arm and made her escape.

THE FINAL EDITION OF THE

EAST PRAIRIE RECORDER

Owen nearly dropped the legal briefs and *Racing Form* when he exited the elevator, finding Nevada Cummings seated in the office lobby. His knees weak, blood rushed from Owen's head upon seeing the man, unsure if Nevada's presence or appearance upset him more.

"Looks like things have turned around, Devonshire. This is much nicer than that last dump." Nevada held an ebony walking stick with both hands, resting his chin on top. "Too bad you still decorate in tacky cowboy."

"Nevada?" Owen's voice sounded weak and shaky. "I'd like to say you're looking well, but why blow hot air up your skirt?"

The old man answered with a laugh, its hearty tone unexpected. He wore the intervening years on his face, a display of depressed cheeks and a spider web of wrinkles.

Formerly-graying afro all but gone, he'd aged a lifetime. His once-dark skin appeared ashen, and the navy business suit swallowed his frail frame, a shroud enveloping a corpse.

"I sent your secretary home for the afternoon. I don't think she much wanted to wait around with me anyway."

"Doesn't surprise me," Owen said, tossing his Stetson on the hat rack. It covered one of the many arms carved into horse heads. "I told her about you years ago."

"Everything?"

"Don't be so smug. I let her know that if you were ever to darken my doorstep, she should clear my schedule for that day." Owen thought the old man's milky blind eye followed his movements better than its healthy counterpart. "I'm sure you're probably here on business, right?"

Nevada struggled free from the leather couch, shuffling toward the office and patting Owen's shoulder as he passed. The man smelled of Old Spice and cigar smoke. His walking stick struck hollow echoes against the hardwood in an ominous rhythm. "It's been seven years, friend. We have a lot of catching up, don't you think?"

Following Nevada, Owen found his way behind the mahogany desk, opening the bottom drawer. He removed a bottle of cognac not touched since Nevada's last visit. The result from that meeting flashed through the lawyer's mind, quickly pushed aside so his guest wouldn't perceive anything amiss.

"So—you dying or what?"

Again, Nevada laughed. "Always to the point. But yes, and I feel worse than I look. The cancer's got me and I'll be gone by year's end—or so your fancy city doctors claim. With what they charge, they surely must be right."

"I'm sorry," Owen said, taken aback that he actually was.

"I bet you are. But you'll miss me after I part ways with this failing body. Whether you wish to admit it or not, we've accomplished quite a lot of good together."

Owen removed a stack of motions from his blotter, balancing them on law books piled in an unsteady conglomeration. He filled two snifters. "Is that so, Nevada?" I thought you'd gone missing out of a crisis of conscience."

"If I didn't know your profession, I'd have guessed you'd be the one struggling with conscience." The old man's good eye steadied on Owen.

Heart accelerating, Owen wondered if Nevada knew, or if his own imagination was reading too much into things. He decided to change the subject. "How's the newspaper business treating you these days?"

"Ah, yes, the *Recorder*. Not much of a paper anymore, I'm afraid. I've only published one special edition since our last business."

Owen silenced another snide remark about conscience before it escaped. Rolling his high-backed chair to the credenza beneath the window with the view of the mountains, he fumbled with the keys before finding the tiny one belonging to the cabinet. "I'd considered throwing these out if I didn't hear from you soon. But something told me you'd be back." He opened the drawer, removing a handful of overstuffed files.

The folders were crammed so tightly, he had to wiggle them free.

"How many you writing this time?"

"Let's not humor ourselves, Devonshire." Nevada produced a thick cigar from his pocket, rolling it between his fingers. "This will be my last issue—my *piece de resistance*—so let's have them all."

"All? Seriously? There's probably a hundred cases in here. Don't you think a rash of my old clients suddenly dropping dead might raise some eyebrows?"

Lighting the cigar, Nevada blew smoke rings across the desk. The latter rings penetrated the earlier, creating a chain effect with the sweet-tinged smoke. "Perhaps, but who'd believe it all anyway? Remember how difficult it was to convince you?"

Owen plopped the first batch of folders and reached for his snifter. "What would you have thought, had you been on my side of that table?"

"I don't know—I wasn't quite convinced it'd work again myself."

The pair had met years earlier at Duffy's Tavern, the unofficial hang out of defense attorneys and public defenders. Owen had been working his way back to his barstool, nose buried in *The Racing Form*, when Nevada slid a chair into the path.

"Congratulations, Devonshire," he'd said. "A beer to celebrate?"

"No thanks, I'm straight."

"And if I were gay, I'd have better taste in men than

you. Sit, please." The grip on Owen's triceps indicated it wasn't so much an invitation as a command. "We need to talk." Owen sat, cautiously taking inventory of the man. Tossing his Stetson on the table, he ordered a Budweiser from the waitress he'd been flirting with all afternoon.

"So what's it feel like to win your first case, Devonshire?"

"Maybe you should start by telling me who the hell you are?" He tried projecting authority, but his words sounded meek. "How do you know my name? About my case?"

Nevada introduced himself as the editor and sole remaining reporter for the *East Prairie Recorder*, a weekly paper headquartered in Seifert—two hours east of Denver. He said he'd been following Owen's first case because of the crime's horrific nature and was concerned that Owen might get his client off due to a technicality. Owen thought he now recognized the stranger from the gallery earlier that morning.

"A technicality? That cop stomped my client's marble bag into mush. Any evidence gained from that confession legally *had* to be thrown out."

"I understand," Nevada said. He sipped his cognac. "Excellent lawyering, I'll add. But how are you going to sleep tonight knowing what crimes your client perpetrated against that boy?"

Owen pushed back from the table, reaching for his hat. "Sorry, Bub. I don't give interviews to reporters."

"Your sense of melodrama will serve you well in your business. But not with me. At least wait for your beer—I have a proposition." Owen remained standing, eyeing the older man with suspicion. "I assure you, I'm not after a story."

Slowly, Owen reclaimed his seat. "Proposition away, but this better be good. I got my eyes on a gelding at Saratoga and twenty minutes to call it in."

"I know you did your job today, but I'm curious as to how. How does it feel knowing you allowed a man who raped a three-year-old to go free?" Nevada's grip clamped on Owen's arm before he could get up again.

The lawyer sighed, beginning with the standard answer preached from the first day of law school. "Everybody's entitled to a fair trial..." But when he looked into Nevada's milky eye, as impersonal as it should appear, Owen found a depth that caught him off guard; a mirror reflecting the suppressed guilt. An unsettling chill ran through him. Eyes welling, his jaw trembled, unable to recite the answer's conclusion. "I'm not the one who did something wrong. It's not like I touched that boy."

"Of course. I've been watching you all week. Your client disgusted you, did he not? You're body language said so—the distance you kept, the way you'd wave him off when he whispered at you."

"Comes with the territory, I guess."

Waving Owen closer, the reporter leaned across the table in a conspirator's crouch. "Listen closely, and don't leave until I've had my say. If then you decide to walk, I promise to never contact you again."

Owen felt like the neighborhood gossip queen about to find out a juicy tidbit on the perfect couple across the street. Nodding for the strange man to continue, his mouth dried in anticipation.

"I can provide that boy justice," Nevada said. Owen sat up strait, shaking his head. "Wait. I promise not to touch your client, and you don't have to do anything but confirm his guilt."

The waitress arrived with Owen's beer and another cognac for Nevada. Thankful for the interruption, Owen drained a large gulp. He watched Nevada remove two wrinkled newspapers from inside the tweed sport coat.

"I've recently come across a unique talent, for lack of a better phrase." He slid one of the papers across the table. "And as God has bestowed upon me this unique ability, I've concluded I must use it for good in some way."

The newspaper headline read:

Prairie Recorder mourns one of its own

The story portrayed the death of Nevada Cumming's wife, 'a peaceful ending to her suffering,' it claimed. She'd apparently died in her sleep after years of enduring some unnamed malady.

"I'm sorry about your wife, but what's this got to do with the price of rice in China?"

"Read the date." Nevada slid the other paper across

the table.

"Week of October sixteenth. This supposed to mean something? I'm growing tired of you being so cryptic. I'm gonna' miss post time."

The second paper was folded to the obituary for Nevada's wife:

Cummings: Emma Maybelline Cummings, 56, passed in her sleep at a friend's home on October 14th. Born in Chicago, she moved to Seifert in 1973 when she and her husband purchased the *East Prairie Recorder*. She is survived by her husband, Nevada Cummings, and a sister, Juliet Alcott of Springfield, IL.

"Look, I said I'm sorry about your wife, but what's all this got to do with me?"

Nevada had been reading the other article as Owen finished the obituary. He wiped the wetness from his eyes, sniffling. "With you? Nothing really, in the final estimation. But I think it could have a great deal to do with your client, and more importantly, that boy he defiled." Nevada sipped his cognac, wetting his lips. "What's the date on that edition?"

"Week of October ninth." It took a moment for the realization to sink in for Owen.

"Emma was suffering something awful. I couldn't stand seeing her in pain anymore, and was spending a good amount of time at the paper. I drank far more than one should, and wrote the obituary as a kind of therapy. Somehow, in my drunken state, I included it in the final edition for that week.

Owen rubbed his temples, wondering how he somehow always attracted the crazies. "Nevada, right? Listen, Nevada, I'm sure this is all a coincidence and I don't see how I fit in this fantasy here. Thanks for the beer. Please accept my condolences—"

"Listen good, Devonshire. Don't take that condescending tone with me. I'm telling you, that obituary had something to do with her demise. Coincidence is having the same name as your bus driver. The obituary named the date of her death, the way she died, and where it happened. Emma hadn't visited that friend in months, and then to die there?"

The discussion continued through two more beers. Owen was never sure if he would have relented had he not been drinking. Whether it had been the booze, Nevada's persistence or his own nagging conscience, he finally admitted that, yes, his client had confessed his guilt—in far too graphic detail for Owen to forget, much less be mistaken.

A week later the rapist was dead, impaled on a chain-link fencepost in a most ironic fashion.

And Owen discovered that indeed, he did sleep better. At first anyway. While he'd convinced himself that was why he continued helping Nevada, he found himself too afraid not to comply; awed by Nevada's gift. Fearing crossing the man, Owen eventually agreed to annual meetings where they'd weed out the worst few cases of the year.

Until Nevada dropped out of sight seven years

earlier, leaving Owen to wonder if the editor did so out of disgust for what they'd done.

"So, you're still betting on the ponies, I see," Nevada said pointing to a copy of *The Racing Form* on Owen's desk. He held out his snifter for a refill.

"Yeah. Still have a soft spot for those of the equine persuasion."

"Ever get around to riding one?"

"I'd prefer to watch from the safety of the betting window." Owen laughed at his own joke.

"Shame. I always found it more fun to participate than to spectate." Owen could tell Nevada was tipsy, the preaching always began once the cognac had loosened him up.

"So, Nevada, this trick of yours—does it work for anything else? Football games?" He emptied the remaining liquor into his own glass. The pair had spent four hours reviewing files, double checking that Owen had confirmed each client's guilt. Scribbles filled Nevada's notebook which would be burned before the paper went to press for its print run of one. "Horse racing, maybe?"

Nevada grinned. "I'm afraid it never applied to any other facet in life but this."

"And after all these years, you've never questioned why? Never felt guilty?" The booze coupled with the realization of this being their last meeting, allowed Owen to talk more freely than usual with Nevada.

"I've questioned why every single day. Every day

concluding it's futile to ask, but asking none-the-less."
Nevada's speech flowed in slurred tones, and Owen
figured the disease had weakened the man's
astonishing tolerance for alcohol. "Guilt was never
much of a factor, but once. You see, Devonshire, we
look at the concept of justice through differing frames
of reference. You view it as something that's supposed
to be administered by the institutions and government
of this country. My experience tells me it's those
institutions and the government that are unjust."

Owen barely heard the sermon part of the answer.
He'd quit paying attention after the confession of guilt
'but once.' Nevada finally noticed Owen's confusion.

"Oh come now, Devonshire. Surely you've known
that I'd figure it out eventually. At first it came as a bit
of relief. When I couldn't find an obituary for any
JoAnna Pearson anywhere, I'd being wondering if I'd
lost my touch. Quite clever using her maiden name.

"But didn't you think I'd notice an obituary with
the last name of 'Devonshire?'"

Knocking over his snifter, Owen cursed as he
reached inside the desk for some napkins.

"I'm sorry, Nevada. Honestly, I am. I've regretted it
every day since, but she was bleeding me dry." The
confession rolled out easily, each word lessening the
burden Owen had carried for years. "I was inches from
bankruptcy, giving all my money away in alimony. She
was buying a house, I was losing my office. I didn't see
another way out." Tossing the soaked napkins in the

waste bin, he again cursed, this time for wasting the last of the cognac. The urge for another drink pulsed through him.

Nevada sat silent, his head shaking like a principal disappointed in a student.

"Don't act so high and mighty with me, Nevada. If I remember, you used your talent to kill your own wife."

"Always the lawyer, aren't you? I think the situations differed greatly."

"Don't be so sure. At our first meeting, you admitted that it was you who couldn't take watching your wife's pain; that she was draining you. Well, JoAnna was draining me, too."

Propping himself using the walking stick, Nevada eased out of the chair. He smoothed his suit and gathered his notepad. "You're a fine lawyer. You have that wonderful ability to mix black and white, and turn everything gray. I almost feel sorry for you."

Owen nearly called out as Nevada walked through the office doorway, out the lobby door to the elevator. He wanted to continue the argument, perhaps to assuage his guilt. But he let the dying man have his final say, feeling lucky it was brief. He'd fretted for seven years what would happen if he ever crossed Nevada's path again, and decided he could live with the results. He'd long ago learned to live with the guilt.

The next few hours, he shredded the files, imagining how Nevada would do in each of the ninety-three former clients. At last, the clean-up done, Owen checked the office for any remaining evidence. As he walked toward the elevator, he noticed something on the lobby couch—a newspaper.

The East Prairie Recorder had a front-page story recounting the annual spring garden show in Seifert. Out of habit, Owen checked the date—the week of April 16, the current week. He flipped to the obituary page

"That sonofabitch."

Cummings: Nevada Cummings, 86, passed away on April 22nd, peacefully in his sleep. He'd just put to bed the final edition of the *East Prairie Recorder* for the week of April 27th...

The obituary comprised half the page, detailing almost every facet of Nevada's life. Except for the part for which Owen knew him best.

As the elevator doors opened, Owen flipped the paper over to the bottom half of the page. His head went woozy when reading the start of the other obituary. He never got past his name as his foot found only air upon entering the vacant elevator shaft

IF MAMA AIN'T

HAPPY

"Don't be scared of me. I got no interest that way." The fat man wiped a hand across his sweatshirt and reached inside the bag of pork rinds. "I remember when Stevie P first brought me out here. That's all I worried about—that he was looking for some of that 'man love.'"

Blinking several times, Clive focused on his new surroundings. The limited light and pain pulsing through his skull hindered his sight. Gagging on an overwhelming stench, he struggled with his breathing, the duct tape covering his mouth. Nothing around him appeared familiar, but for certain he hadn't reached Graceland.

"You just relax, partner. We can make this as hard or as easy-peazy as you want." The man gulped off his Nehi, some of the sticky fluid escaping the sides of his mouth and down his chin. Setting the soda on a cinder block coffee table, he clicked on the thirteen-inch Sony resting on a TV tray. An infomercial appeared—make a fortune in real estate with no money down—but the volume was off. "Mama ain't going to be ready till midnight or so. She's probably feeding her rug-rats. You just lay low here, and it'll all be over before you can whistle Dixie."

By the television's glow, the décor of the cramped trailer materialized. Dark faux-wood paneling shrouded the walls, and a worn path ran through the linoleum from the kitchen to the screen door. The irony not lost on Clive, a velvet Elvis painting hung misaligned over the television.

He thought he glimpsed a silhouette of a head peeking through the screen, but when he blinked, nothing was there. The full-moon's shimmer revealed only the strange mounds outside.

"Mama's gonna love you—young, a little meat on your bones. Not like that skinny bastard, Stevie P. I can't believe they ever..." The fat man shook his head and downed the remaining orange drink, tossing the empty bottle into an overflowing bin. "But she's with me now and that's what matters."

A rustling sounded from the kitchen, followed by a crash. Tin cans rolled across the linoleum.

"Get outta there, you little shits and shitters!" The fat man stomped, rocking the trailer like a rusted-out Camero on shot springs.

Feet scurried across the kitchen floor. Clive struggled to sit up, but the tape binding his arms threw him off balance and he toppled sideways with a thud. A shadow, the size of a large dog, motored on all fours, waddling across the doorway. Thrashing about, the tape muffled Clive's screams. Whichever drug he'd been slipped was wearing off.

The fat man punched him dead in the forehead. "Don't go getting no ideas. You'll only make this harder on yourself."

Tensing his body, Clive stopped squirming. He inhaled, calming himself as the pain from the blow and his anger hastened his emergence from the drug-induced stupor. Nodding, he acknowledged the fat man's instructions.

"That's better. Don't go doing that again—I don't want to hurt you." The fat man paced the tiny room, shooing away buzzing insects. "I hate this part. Makes it hard to sleep sometimes. I keep tellin' myself, 'Vernon, you gotta get outta this somehow.' But I know I never will. Love makes you do some crazy shit, you know?"

Clive mumbled beneath the duct tape.

"You want that off, do you?"

Clive nodded emphatically.

"S'pose it won't hurt none. Even if you screamed like a school girl at a slasher movie, there ain't much out this way to hear you." The fat man yanked free the tape, ripping away several mustache hairs. "Except for Mama and them damn kids. The crazy ones usually steer clear of my trailer, though. Keep to their own turf." He winked and patted Clive hard on the shoulder before shuffling back to his decaying La-Z-Boy.

"Where am I?" He doubled over, coughing from the heavy stench.

"I'd guess a long way from home. You one of them

English pussies?"

"What?" Clive, clenching his hands, glared at his captor. He pictured wrapping them around the fat man's neck blubber. "What is this place? Who the bloody hell are you?"

"Calm down there—don't get your knickers in a knot. That's how you English chaps say it, right?" He removed his worn Atlanta Braves cap from his shaved head and bowed. The motion was exaggerated, mockingly. "Vernon G. Largess at your service. But we met already."

A river of thoughts, anger, and confusion rushed through Clive. He nibbled his bottom lip, forcing himself into a calm state. Lately, his emotions had dictated his actions far too much, and going off half-cocked was partially responsible for putting him in this position. That and the promise he made to his mother that someday he'd visit Graceland because she had always dreamed of going herself.

"Guess you probably didn't pay much attention to a local yokel like me, but I picked you up at the airport." A devilish grin crept across Vernon's face. "Remember?"

"I can't recall much of anything." Which was true. He couldn't really recollect boarding the plane in London, but the Bloody Marys accounted for that.

"You called for a cab and I answered. That taxi's the one good thing Stevie P left. Makes it a butt-load easier to get folks when Mama's ready." He dug for another pork rind, popping it in his mouth. "I slipped you a little ether cocktail, and you was agreeable as a drunken prom queen."

Clive struggled to a sitting position, the tape cutting into his wrists. He looked to the screen door. The garbage mounds offered plenty of hiding places, but with his feet and hands bound...

"Don't even think about it," Vernon said. "Even if you got past me, Mama's kids would tear you up before you got ten steps out the door. 'Specially if you ran into some of Stevie P's. They's some aggressive fuckers, let me tell you."

Assessing the situation, Clive agreed running—or hopping—away would only aggravate the circumstances. "Vernon, is it? What do you want of me? I'm due for a crucial merger negotiation tomorrow— I'm sure to be missed," he lied. In fact, nobody knew where he was. Once Clive finally decided staying together for the kids was no longer worth enduring Emily's infidelity, he simply up and left. Instead of turning right to the office, he took a left to the pub, and in a drunken rage decided it was time he'd finally seen Elvis' home. No notice to the firm, no note to the family. He wanted to get as far away as possible, and although quite by accident, he'd now succeeded more than he could've imagined.

"They'll be looking for me soon. You won't get away—p"

Vernon guffawed, spraying Nehi like a sticky

sprinkler. "I'll worry about that...seems you should have other concerns right about now. But, I don't want nothing from you. Just wanna keep Mama happy." He inhaled another swig. The chorus from *That's Alright Mama* ran through Clive's thoughts.

"When her urges start a-flowin', it gets my hackles up a bit, you know?" Vernon bent as far as his flab allowed, lowering his voice. "I wasn't a bad guy, honest. Don't get me wrong. I'm a bad guy now—done some downright awful shit—but I wasn't before Stevie P dragged my ass out here."

Clive squirmed, searching for a comfortable position. "But who's Mama? I assure you I've never met—"

"You will." Vernon nestled into the chair, a plume of dust escaping as his weight readjusted. "I wouldn't be in too big a rush if I was you."

Clive recalled seeing a television program claiming the best chance for a kidnap victim to survive was to keep the captor engaged. He grasped for anything to continue the conversation.

"Who's this Stevie P you keep mentioning?"

Vernon chuckled as if the question were too complex to answer. "Sit back there, Nigel—"

"Actually it's Clive."

"Whatever. Sit back and I'll tell you a thing or two about Stevie P. Help kill the time anyway." Vernon dusted the pork rind crumbs from his hands. "I'd known Stevie P since we was both sucking titties for breakfast. His real name was Steven SomefuckinIndianname. He was Apache or Seminole, I think. Like I said, some fuckin' Indian. But we all called him Stevie P because that little cuss wet his pants 'til he was nine or so. Swear to God."

Vernon shifted in the La-Z-Boy, releasing a wet fart. The chair moaned. The sight disgusted Clive, but he maintained his calm demeanor, concealing his desire to break the fat fuck's neck. He hoped he'd get the chance to show what a pissed off 'pussy Englishman' could really do.

"Stevie P was a squirrelly little sum-bitch. Strange as a two-headed ass, too—always praying and wearin' all sorts of jewelry. I knew he was queer from the minute I knew what queer was."

Vernon's discharge wafted across the room, its vapors adding to the miasma. The nauseating pall hung over Clive, sharp and repulsive, watering his eyes.

"I'd forgot all about the little fucker until he walks into the Riverside Tavern about twenty years later. He had a wad of cash and started buying me drinks. Next thing I remember, I'm waking up in the back of this cab, tied up right like you. I tell you what, I was glad I came to on my back. I was going to protect my hindquarters at all costs. Exit only, you know."

Outside an uproar erupted. Clive thought it a fight between two alley cats, but the cries consisted of deeper, more boisterous wails. Vernon reached behind his La-Z-Boy and removed a rusted sawed-off shotgun.

"Damn kids," he said. "I'll be right back." He pried himself from the chair and thundered out the door, beyond Clive's sight. A shot exploded. "Stop it, you little fuckers! So help me, if y'all are Stevie P's, I'll skin you half alive."

What have I done? Clive thought. Memories of his girls, Priscilla and Lisa Marie, filled his mind. He mentally kicked himself for following his impulse to leave. If he hadn't, he'd probably be picking the girls up from school now instead of in this crazy predicament.

He stretched, trying to see through the grimy screen, and spied Vernon's elongated shadow in the moonlight with the shotgun resting on a shoulder. Another shadow, similar to the one he'd seen in the kitchen, scampered over the trash heaps. Clive's shoulder popped from the stress. Closing his eyes, he fought the pain, but lost his balance.

Another shot cracked through the night, followed by screeches that burrowed into Clive's spine. He rolled off the couch, his shoulder aching. Like a worm, he slowly inched toward the door.

"Y'all are mighty rambunctious tonight, ain't cha?" Vernon yelled. "You best get more organized if you think you can take me. I'll kill the lot of ya' and fry you up for breakfast—tails and all!"

Clive crossed the grungy linoleum to the door and propped himself up on his elbow. At the base of the garbage mound, a Labrador-sized beast scurried away, a rat-like tail dragging behind through the dirt. It reared up on its back legs and sprinted with an awkward gait into the horizon of waste.

Vernon lumbered back to the trailer, shotgun in tow. Clive rolled back to the couch, his heart thudding. He wasn't sure what frightened him more—the alien animal or Vernon. He rested his head on the cushion, his energy too sapped to get back on the broken-down furniture.

The screen door slammed shut behind Vernon. His smugness revealed itself through his smile as he hovered over Clive.

"Going somewhere?"

"What the hell was that? Is that one of the children?"

Vernon reached down as Clive cowered against the sofa. "Yup, I think that was one of mine. Stevie P's are skinnier." He picked Clive up by his belt and deposited him back on the moldy cushions. "His'n mine got one hell of a turf war going on now."

The blood rushed from Clive's head. He wished the Ether had never begun wearing off. Instinctively, he attempted to stand.

Extending a beefy arm, Vernon pointed the shotgun. "I highly recommend you sit your limey ass down. I thought with all them fancy English manners, you'd understand I'm in the middle of a story here. It'd be downright rude to make me kill you before I finish."

Clive gritted his teeth, glaring at his captor. He looked at the barrel and slowly lowered himself back on the couch. Vernon removed a shell from his pocket, reloading the shotgun.

Outside, a call, close to a mewling dropped from the sky and washed over the trailer. Bumps grew on Clive's arms and the hair rose as if excited by static. The call sounded like a train horn in distress, deep and strident.

Vernon rested the shotgun on his shoulder and picked up his half-finished Nehi. "Looks like I'll have to finish our story along the way. You got a date with Mama."

Clive's feet slipped on the linoleum as he backed away into the couch. "Stay away! I don't know what sickness you've been carrying on—"

Vernon slammed the shotgun's butt into Clive's abdomen. The blow knocked the air from him, dropping him to his knees.

"I don't think you're in much of a position to judge me. Now, on your feet, sissy-boy." Leaning over him, Vernon pulled him up by one arm. He bent Clive over his shoulder and waddled to the door. "It's time you met Mama."

The taxi was a run-down minivan with balding tires and a crumpled front fender. Vernon threw Clive in the back seat, slamming the door shut. The cab's frame creaked when Vernon entered. It shifted with a series of groans and pops, tilting toward the driver's side.

"Now keep your yapper shut," Vernon whispered. The cab started after several tries, spewing plumes of foul, oil-choked smoke. Pulling a U-turn, Vernon followed a dirt road around the trailer. "We got to go over to the north sector, but we pass through some pretty rough spots. With the turf war and all, this might get hairy. Don't do anything to draw their attention, or we'll be in for a brawl

"I lost some dumbfuck when I didn't tie his feet good enough. He busted out and ran for it right about here. Little fuckers ripped him to pieces."

"Please, don't do whatever you have planned. I have two girls at home that need me."

Vernon eyed him through the rear-view mirror. Clive believed he detected a hint of mercy. "I can't help you there, Nigel. Mama needs you, too."

Clive's chest hammered and he worried he might suffer a heart attack. He wondered if Emily had reported him missing—or cared at all—but doubted the cavalry was on its way. The landfill's stench burned his lungs. He coughed, his eyes watering.

"Button it up, will ya?" The cab crept along, finding every possible rut.

"These things?" Clive asked in a whisper. "These creatures are your children?"

"Some of 'em. I quit counting 'round two-hundred."

Clive sank against the seat, his head bouncing along with the van. Vernon inserted a cassette into the player, and the one working speaker spat out *In the Ghetto*. Shaking his head, Clive couldn't believe he'd been kidnapped by a fellow Elvis devotee. He felt somehow betrayed.

The moon backlit the drifts of garbage. As he focused, Clive saw the outline of several of the 'kids' milling over the landscape. He nearly cried from fear.

"But where was I with Stevie P?"

"In the back of the taxi," Clive answered, barely recognizing that he'd spoken.

"Oh yeah—right, like you now. Anyways, Stevie P brought me out to the north sector for my meeting with Mama. He tied me all up and shit, but I guess with my size it was a might harder to cinch down the knots. There was this plywood plank rigged up on some little wheels—he called it an altar, but it looked like a moldy piece of plywood to me. Anyway, he knelt me on this thing, but all I saw was Mama.

"You believe in love at first sight, Nigel?"

"It's Clive, and no, I don't."

"Whatever." Vernon tapped the breaks as the van wound down a hill. "I never gave it no thought, neither, but I fell for Mama right on the spot. I got lost in those big brown eyes like they spoke to me saying all the right things. I felt all dreamy, didn't even remember where I was. I think I just wanted to hold her, you know? When I tried bringing my arms up, the ropes somehow slipped off. I pushed myself up to run, but forgot about the job Stevie P did on my feet. I lost my balance and fell back on that sorry Indian sum-bitch. I think I broke his fucking back.

"Mama got her panties all in a bunch then,

screaming and thrashing around like she had a bath in itchin' powder. I felt awful, like I'd hurt her somehow. But, like magic, I understood all what she was saying. She don't speak no English, and I ain't a man of many languages, but I could talk to her—like she put the words right in my head. I just knew, by instinct, what I had to do."

A deafening bang sounded on the roof, and the van shuddered. "You little sum-bitches!" Vernon yelled, slamming on the brakes.

Sliding from the van's roof, the creature's paws scraped across the hood sounding like nails scraping against the metal. It bounced on the hood, buckling the steel, and plunged to the dirt road. Clive smashed into the front seat before recoiling against the back.

The thing rose on its squat hind legs. In the headlights, Clive saw that it was covered in dark, matted fur except its face. It appeared human around the ears and eyes, but displayed an elongated snout and needle-like teeth protruded from its mouth. The headlights reflected off the eyes, making them appear as floating, soulless orbs. The creature raised both arms, the rodent-like hands balled in fists with tufts of fur poking through sharp fingers. It stood about four feet and was much thinner than the shadows Clive'd seen before. Rushing toward the cab, it tittered an angry exclamation.

His body frozen with fear, Clive gazed in warped fascination. It seemed like a bad acid trip from college come to life. If not for the pain ripping through his arms, he'd have thought it all a terrible nightmare. And in one of those inappropriate flashes the mind tosses out, he wondered what Emily and the girls were doing.

"That ain't good," Vernon said. He punched the gas. The rat-thing splintered the windshield and bounced out of view.

"What? What's not good?" Clive turned, looking out the back window. Dozens of the creatures chased the van, running with the swift gait of a rodent and pouncing with each step. Clive bit his tongue, repressing a scream.

"That was one of Stevie P's. This is s'posed to be my kids' territory." Clive nearly laughed. Elvis crooned the chorus of *In the Ghetto*, through the speaker.

Another creature rammed the front of the van, rocking the vehicle. Swarms emerged from the trash heaps as if the garbage spewed them forth.

A rush of rank wind assaulted Clive as Vernon cranked down the driver-side window. While steering with his right hand, he extended his left arm, pulling the shotgun's trigger. Clive jumped at the piercing blast, seeing one of the creatures drop as the lead shot exploded its skull. The pursuing horde scattered, heading back to the safety of the trash heaps. Vernon drove a while longer before slowing the cab back to a crawl.

"Frisky tonight, ain't they?" Vernon's voice shook. "I told you Stevie P's was some aggressive fuckers."

"What's it mean?" Clive asked, his tone quivering. "Them being in your kids' territory?"

"The turf war's taken a turn. Anything could happen tonight."

Clive granted the pent-up tears a release. He berated himself. Why had he, the steady father, the faithful husband, the even-keeled citizen, suddenly acted on impulse and hopped on a plane to America, not even understanding where Graceland was. I shouldn't be here at all.

His wrists struggled against the duct tape. He wanted one shot at Vernon before this ended.

"What does Mama want with me?" he asked, knowing he wouldn't like the answer.

"It's the full moon. She needs another man. Not that way—I got her all taken care of there." Vernon put his finger to one nostril, blowing free a hunk of mucus. "I'm not sure why, but that's all she really asks from me. I think Stevie P did something with all that Indian juju to turn her into what she is now. It's the only thing I've come up with that makes any sense. Not that it makes much sense, but it's the best I've been able to figure, anyway. I think it was some downright evil shit, if you ask me."

Clive struggled for breath, unable to stop the tears. If he hadn't seen the strange offspring, he wouldn't believe a word Vernon had said.

"If it makes you feel any better, they all seem to enjoy it. I can't explain, but even Stevie P flopped

SLIGHTLY OFF-CENTER / 191

around with a big ol' smile across his face. I remember Mama ripping away his insides and him chanting some Indian gibberish all the while. Damnedest thing I ever saw."

The van rounded a bend, revealing another clearing nestled among surrounding piles of garbage. The mounds undulated. Creatures swam over each other making the heaps appear alive.

Clive watched in horror, the events not fully registering in his mind. He still half expected to wake up outside the gates of The King's Memphis home; Vernon, his kids, and the impending meeting with Mama all nothing but some alcohol-induced dream.

In the moonlight, he saw the altar. It rested in front of a mound the size of a bi-level house. The mound appeared different, obviously not comprised of trash. The van drawing closer, Clive noticed the enormous attachment at the back of the mound. A good thirty feet long, it tapered to a fine point. The attachment flicked up, and Clive realized it was a tail. Then he saw the elongated nose and the gigantic rodent teeth when Mama tilted her head for a better view of the approaching taxi.

Clive screamed, thrashing about as if trying to escape his own skin. Kicking the front seat, he knocked Vernon into the horn. It blared and startled the brood feeding from Mama. They turned their attention to the van, some raised on hind legs for a better look. Several scrambled about, pacing in skittish steps. Hissing and tittering filled the air as they formed a gauntlet of vermin.

Vernon punched the brakes and slammed the Nehi across Clive's temple. "Stop it! You're gonna make it worse."

Clive leaned his head against the front seat. Blood and sticky soda stung his eyes. His thoughts flashed to images of Priscilla and Lisa Marie. He'd defined himself as a father, but allowed jealousy to cloud what was important. If he'd somehow escape this, he vowed, he'd return home immediately—Graceland be damned. Surely there was still hope for him and Emily—at least for the girls' sake.

"No. No fuckin' way," Vernon said. He jammed the gearshift into park, opening his door with a great thrust. Waddling around the front of the van, he mumbled "no" along the way, and opened the door with a yank.

"Get out, sissy-boy." Vernon reached inside and pulled Clive out with one arm. He tossed him to the ground as if he weighed no more than a house cat. "Stay here. I'll beat you silly if you don't. You keep quiet why I take care of some business."

He raised the shotgun, firing into the mounds. "This ain't over, you little fuckers! Me and Mama can always make more, ya' hear?" He fired again.

Clive rolled on his side to find a score or more of the fatter children pile in a pyramid—all obviously dead. Tasting bile, he swallowed back the vomit rising in his throat. Vernon continued screaming threats while blubbering in sobs. He backed toward Clive, reaching into his pocket for more shells.

Mama cried again, the mewling reverberating through Clive's skeleton. He heard the melancholy in the call, and it bought an ache to his heart. Grinding his teeth, he let his anger—with Vernon, with himself— rise.

"I'll shoot all of you tonight if I have to!" A shell dropped to the ground. Vernon took two steps back, grunting as he reached for it.

Adrenaline coursed through Clive, his ears ringing. "It's now or never," he sang in his best Elvis voice as he coiled back his legs. With his captor's backside within reach, he sprang both feet into the broad target of Vernon's ass, knocking him forward. Unable to stop his momentum, the American cracked his head against the open van door, collapsing to the ground in a heap of moaning blubber.

Stevie P's brood seized their opportunity, flowing from the heaps like a river of vindictive vermin. Vernon screamed when the first rat-thing pounced. Several others piled on as Mama released another haunting cry. The poignant tones mingled with Vernon's screams, harmonizing into an ungodly chorus.

Clive's body shook as he fixated on the scene. Focusing on the carnage, he barely noticed when one of the kids began gnawing through the duct tape. The sound of blood rushed through his head, thrumming to the beat of an off-kilter drummer. Dizzy, he found calmness when he focused on Mama's mating call. He finally noticed the creature working at the tape around his legs. Hate glared at him through the rat-thing's eyes, but Clive somehow understood he wouldn't be harmed. He heard it in Mama's melodious cries.

When Mama's call stopped, the melee ceased. An eerie silence surrounded the landfill, Clive hearing only the thudding of his heart. The creatures backed away from Vernon, who rolled about languidly. Maintaining eye contact with Clive, the creatures slowly receded, obviously disappointed they were called off before finishing with Vernon. Some backed away on two legs, others on four, back to their turf. Clive felt them evaluating him, summing him up. Empathetic toward them, he understood what it was like to have some strange man wrestle away a valuable part in your life—whether it be stealing your wife or replacing your father.

He turned to Mama. Her eyes were the size of his head, brown and glassy. Staring into their benevolence for a long while, motionless, he saw her pain, her need for somebody—anybody but Vernon. She injected her memories of hate for the fat man, and by instinct, Clive understood what must be done. With his family in tatters, he willingly accepted the role she asked of him.

He rolled Vernon, his body a swollen bag of oatmeal, onto the altar and pushed it closer to Mama. It glided smoothly over the gravel, guided by some other force. Once the altar was close enough, Clive stepped away and gazed at the marvelous creature before him. He smiled, spreading his arms to present the offering.

"Yes, Mama," he answered her unspoken question. "It's Clive. No, not Nigel—Clive."

Mama dug into her meal proving Vernon right. The fat man massaged his chest, moaning with joy. A delirious smile twisted his face.

A part of Clive's subconscious needled at him like an annoying gnat. He thought there was something else he must do, something he was forgetting. But when he looked at Mama again, the gnat disappeared. He knew he was home.

Hearing the squishing sounds of Mama eating, he ambled toward her distended midsection, whistling *Love Me Tender*. He nestled at a teat. An erection grew and he buried it into Mama's flesh. Sucking in her milk, he moaned in ecstasy. He snuggled as close as possible, kicking away some of her feeding offspring.

He would wait for her to finish her meal before consummating their new arrangement.

DISH TIME

He went to remove the gold-plated wedding ring. Purchased only two days before, it was a half-size too small, but with his fat fingers it was as close to a fit as they could find.

You leave that on. Don't you dare take it off.

What?

Never.

Never?

Well, you can take it off when I clean it for you. You can take it off when I die, but you're my man and that's our ring, and you wear it always.

Always? I'll leave it on this time, but always?

Dish time, Sausage.

Jane pointed to the sink, reached into the suds and grabbed a handful, blew them into the air. Giggled like a happy newlywed that was all Sausage wanted her to be with every cell in every fiber of his ever-loving being. Laughed like the music of the Andrews Sisters or Benny Goodman or Satchmo. Laughed as to tell him everything was all right and would always be all right because that was all it needed to be.

Next time, too. Dish time, next time, and always.

Sausage also laughed, couldn't help himself. Maybe not next time, but dish time.

He cut off the water. Suds rose from the sink in a mountain of bubbles that begged to be jumped in.

Bubbles that held promise. Everything held promise.

Jane turned up the Motorola and sang along with Bob Hope to *Thanks for the Memories,* on The Pepsodent Show. She held their cigarette to his lips for his turn. He didn't really/truly inhale any smoke, it was too awkward, but it was nice.

You're really going to wear that all night?

I waited for two years while you were in that war. I'm going to wear this dress until the seams pop out.

You're going to get it wet, you know.

Yes, and it has a wine stain, and the train is covered in dirt from our dirty floors. But they're our dirty floors, and it's my dress, and I'm a classy broad who likes to wear a dress around the apartment.

But that one?

Especially this one.

You're silly.

I'm brilliant.

Yes, that's it. Sorry, sometimes I get confused.

I know, but I love you still.

Sausage bent to kiss Jane. Her kiss was soft and ephemeral and heavenly. Her kiss was like air.

He started washing, sank his hands into the steamy water and suds almost too hot for his bare skin. The task wouldn't take long since they owned but two plates, but two saucers, but two bowls—all hard plastic with a sunflower pattern. Jane had cashed in her Green Stamps for them.

We won't have to do this long. Once I start

working, I'm going to buy you one of them Electrolux machines. The fancy ones.

To hell you are.

Such language. And from such a classy broad.

Can you ever forgive me?

Dish time. Maybe not next time, but dish time.

They both laughed. They'd always really/truly laughed in their times together. He knew there'd be lots of it in the years ahead. He'd missed laughing. Heard little of it in Korea. Done less of it.

You're such a gentleman, Sausage. A manly gentleman with manly arms and a manly heart, but I don't want any damn dishwashing machine. Not as long as we live and we get this time to ourselves.

I don't think I'll ever understand you.

Yes. Sometimes you get confused.

Yes, I do.

He desperately wanted a drag off the cigarette, but Jane had seemed to have forgotten to share.

Can we at least have a television?

Of course, Sausage.

I just want you to be happy.

I'll be happy with you. Jane took a puff off the Pall Mall. And happy if you let me die first. Promise me that. I couldn't live with you dying on me. I had to worry about that every day for two years.

Sausage shrugged. What's that have to do with a television?

Jane grew quiet for a moment. Turned her gaze.

Smoothed the dress over the wine stain.

Fine. I can't do nothing about it, but I promise.

Jane allowed a sneaky smile. And yes, we can have a television for every room and a fleet of Studebakers and big houses and...

I'd settle for a television right now.

Right now, I'll settle for another glass of wine. Jane walked out of the apartment's kitchen, Pall Mall in tow, for the bottle she'd left in the dining/living/bedroom. She was gone for a long while.

Sausage missed her. Really/truly missed her. The house seemed dark without her. Empty.

The fists pounded on him like hail. Cold. Hard strikes from such delicate hands with no purpose but to land, but he knew he deserved them. Deserved every last stinking blow. Every hurtful surreal blow because he wasn't the man he'd promised he'd be.

You missed a spot

He looked down to the red ceramic plate and saw remnants of Rice-O-Roni stubbornly sticking.

How'd you see that from there?

Pregnancy eyes. I have superpowers.

You're silly.

I'm brilliant.

That's right. Sometimes I get confused.

Yes, you do.

Jane sat at the kitchen table, smoking her Pall Mall and drinking her wine while watching *Bonanza* on the living-room TV. She was too pregnant to stand for long, so Sausage did the dishes alone, but she sat in the kitchen with him every night. Sat and talked and pecked and complimented and asked.

He picked free a grain of rice stuck in his wedding ring and dried his hands.

You want me to clean that for you? The ring.

What? And get rid of all the luck?

Isn't it starting to smell?

Sausage held his hand to his face. His fingers were thick, the reason she'd first started calling him by the nickname. Although, back in Korea, then at the plant, he'd suspected his friends called him it for a different reason. He sniffed the ring finger. Waved and wafted his hands as if taking in the aroma of a fine wine. Grinned so Jane understood he was joking.

No smell. Not dish time.

Maybe next time.

They laughed out of habit. They did that a lot. That part was nice, still. Still.

You going to wear that all day?

What else can I fit in?

Jane wore nothing but a quilt wrapped around her under a terrycloth bathrobe that had long ago seen better days.

You think I'm hideous. You don't like me in this.

I like you in anything.

Jane smiled. Glowed. Lit up the kitchenette against the backdrop of Hoss and Little Joe.

You're a good man, Sausage. You're full of shit, but

a good man.

Such language from such a classy broad.

Yes. That's how I feel right now. A fat, classy broad.

Sausage scrubbed the pots with an SOS pad. Tried thinking of something to lighten the situation.

You get Holly her birthday present?

Yes. I had to go to two different places to find that damn Barbie.

Such language from such a classy broad. Sausage didn't know what else to say.

You're used to it by now.

I am.

And he really/truly was.

He looked to the clock, realized he'd have to be to the plant in an hour. The shift differential helped in a lot of ways, but he hated not being home for Jane and Holly. What kind of man is gone all night to leave his pregnant wife and young daughter alone? Thunderbirds weren't going to build themselves, though, were they? Union meetings weren't going to run themselves, were they?

I wish I could help. Jane patted her inflated belly.

You just sit there and take care of my son.

I'm telling you, it's not a boy. A mother can tell.

It better be a boy. You got your daughter, now we need a little manliness around this house.

You're manly enough for us all.

Sausage flexed his biceps like Charles Atlas. Dishwater splashed everywhere. You're probably right.

Upstairs, a thud. Sausage and Jane looked at each other, the obligatory silent countdown in their heads. Before they reached five, Holly's wails started. Jane scooted to the chair's edge, placed one hand on the table, the other on the seat, rocked a couple of times, and pushed herself up, pregnancy bump first.

I'll be back before you go to work.

She waddled down the hallway and disappeared up the stairs. She was gone for a long while, and Sausage missed her. More than he could take.

—

Behind him, the front door opens and closes. For a moment, he catches reality, but it escapes on frenzied fleet feet.

—

He continued washing the fondue pot. Beneath the soapy water, a fork jabbed him. He pulled his hand free of the cooling water, the long fondue fork, the orange one, stuck beneath his wedding ring. Jane guffawed. Jane was a little drunk, but it was okay. It was her night.

You're going to wear that forever?

I'm going to wear it until the university finds out I stole it. Don't you like me in a mortarboard?

I like you in anything.

Jane smiled a hurt smile, and the silence was awkward and awful, and there'd been a lot of it lately. It really/truly wasn't nice. He couldn't look at her. She sipped more of her wine.

I'm proud of you, you know.

Thank you, Sausage.

I mean it. It's a good example for Holly and Marsha. It was a lot of work, but you did it. It's amazing.

Don't try so hard.

I'm not.

You are.

In the other room, on the Curtis Mathis, Carol Burnett lost her composure at something Tim Conway had said or done, and it was apparently hilarious. Sausage couldn't hear it too well, though. Not over the water and the muted Partridge Family song that Marsha played non-stop in her room upstairs.

You decide on which hospital you'll work at?

Stop. It doesn't matter. You're trying so hard.

I just want to make it up to you.

You can't.

I know.

She reached to touch his hand, but stopped. Her near touch was beautiful and ethereal and would have been heavenly. It was like air sucked from his lungs.

I'll forgive you, though. Dish time, I'll forgive you.

Why?

Because you're a good man, Sausage. You give us a good home. Because I think I love you. Because for better or worse, in sickness and health.

Good men don't do what I did.

No. Some good men make mistakes, though. Don't make it again, okay? Jane's eyes swelled with tears she wouldn't allow to escape.

I couldn't. Don't be silly.

You're confused—I'm brilliant.

Yeah, sometimes I get that way. You're too good for me, you know?

Yes. I'm a way classier broad than you deserve.

Jane put her empty wine glass in the sudsy water, picked some of the sagging suds up and blew them into the air where they popped like dreams. She left to make sure Marsha had completed her homework. She was gone for a long while. Sausage missed her so much his chest ached. His mind spun. His soul deflated.

Still, the blows came. Over and over and over and over. Warranted, but that made them no less painful. In sickness and in health. Made them no less of a surprise. For better or worse.

—

"You think he knows we're here?" he hears the youngest one say.

—

You going to wear that all night?

Hell yes. How many mothers are asked to be Maids of Honor in their daughter's wedding?

Wedding. It rang a bell. In the background some asshole sung something about a White Wedding. He wished he could start again.

Such language. You are no classy broad.

Classier than you deserve.

Jane was right. And looked spectacular in her

brides' maid dress, despite its inherent poor taste.

She inhaled from an imagined Pall Mall, having quit that particular habit after getting her nurse's certificate, and blew invisible imagined smoke rings at him.

You're silly.

Maybe. But I'm mostly brilliant.

Can you be one or the other? I get confused.

The DJ called Sausage to the floor for the father/daughter dance, but Sausage, for the life of him, couldn't remember which daughter. Couldn't really/truly remember how many he had. He walked to the floor and hoped the right one would find him. Smiled, determined to show the guests nothing was amiss. He recognized the Nat King Cole tune, but wondered who the female was that sang in the duet.

One daughter found him. He knew her name started with an H. Hoped her name did, anyway. Hoped she was his daughter. He danced like he hadn't a care.

Jane walked to the bar for more wine. Disappeared into the night. Sausage missed her so much, his heart fell into disrepair.

He couldn't protect himself. He raised his hands over his head, but beautiful fists crashed in waves of fury, accompanied with cries of anguish, shards of a broken heart, and he accepted defeat.

—

"Give him a chance. It's got to be rough."

—

Jane, it's time to take that outfit off.

She wore all black. A short-sleeve dress showed the freckles gone awry on her arms. A veil. Long gloves.

Never.

Never?

Don't you see? Can't you see?

Sorry, sometimes I get confused.

Damn right you do.

But Sausage remembered the tiny coffin lowered into the ground. Remembered he should have been stronger. Remembered how much he didn't remember.

Jane threw the wine cork at him.

A classy broad wouldn't do that. A classy broad wouldn't have to.

On the TV above the bar, an odd chase scene played out. A Bronco, but he couldn't remember anybody named Simpson playing for the Broncos, ran away from the police. It looked nothing like football, but Sausage knew somehow it had something to do with football.

"I can't take this, Sausage. I'm supposed to die first, remember? You promised." Somewhere, he thought that particular memory might exist. Didn't know what it had to do with the tiny coffin, but knew some connection was there for him not to find.

Jane had locked herself in the bathroom, and he missed her. Despite it all, he missed her more than anything. Missed what should have been. What he couldn't fix now.

He fell asleep on the couch. In the fetal position,

hands over his head, protecting himself from the blows to come later. He did that a lot lately. It wasn't nice.

—

"Is he okay?"

Sausage knows they stand behind him. He could see Holly—knows that's her name—cuddling with her decapitated Barbie, it naked as it has been almost from the first day she got it. Marsha—the nice one—in pigtails, her one dimple shining as she giggles at anything anybody says. And then pictures them as Hannah—knows it's her name, wearing tie-dye, about to tell him that she's quitting school, and Mary in a cheerleading outfit asking for a ride to the freshman game. And then as Heather—that's her name, right?— with the dark cloud that's followed her since the baby died, and Miriam as he escorts her down the aisle in the dress that her mother wore, complete with wine stain.

He won't turn to look. Doesn't want them to see him like this. He's too manly for that.

—

He set the Tupperware in the other side of the sink to dry. In the background, Fox News told him some black man had ruined the country he'd fought for in Korea.

So, you're really going to wear that?

I wear it to take care of people with infantile minds, why wouldn't I wear it here? Jane opened another bottle of wine.

Sausage flinched when the cork popped. Sudden movements, loud sounds, scared him.

But you're not at work, Jane.

It's always work, Sausage. You're a lot of work.

I know. Sometimes I get confused.

No shit.

Please, Jane, watch the language.

Jane just stood and watched him at the sink. Sausage rubbed the scab on his cheek, the one from her wedding ring. Hoped she wasn't drunk enough to leave another.

There sure are a lot of glasses to wash.

Yes.

Wine glasses.

Well, I'm a classy broad. And this classy broad drinks her wine out of a glass. It's classy.

It's a lot of glasses.

I drink a lot of wine.

I'm sorry about that.

Yes. Me, too.

It's just...

I know, Sausage. Sometimes you get confused. Sometimes you forget. You get to forget. So, sometimes I like wine so I can forget, too.

Yeah. Sometimes I get confused, but not dish time.

Jane smiled. Not in joy. In resignation. She took another drink, from her glass, because she was classy.

Dish time, too.

Why would you want to forget? I just want to remember.

Because it's hard. It's so damn hard.

I don't do it on purpose.

Me either.

I know.

I love you, you know? Really/truly.

I love you, too. But it's so damn hard. You said I could die first.

I meant it then. Really/truly.

Jane went upstairs to go to bed. She'd been gone for a long, long, long, eternal while. And Sausage missed her so much.

———

Behind him, the front door opens and shuts again.

"Grandpa, it's time to go." Ally or Amy or Amanda, something like that, twirls her key ring around her middle finger. She stands behind Marsha or Mindy or Mary and Holly or Hilda or Harry. They're older than he remembers, but he doesn't remember much.

The dishwater feels cold—used up. He removes the last plate and holds it out for inspection. The sight of his hands catches him off guard. They're old and wrinkled and dappled with brown age spots and his ring finger displays a permanent indention where the old, gold-plated ring used to be.

He hands the plate to Jane to dry, but it slips. It breaks on the floor. "Oh, dear. Your mother is going to be so mad."

"Dad, stop it," Holly or Harriet or Hannah says. She's in full make-up. In a black dress, and Sausage hasn't seen her in a dress in years. Not that he could remember anyway. "The nurses will clean it up, okay?"

"Your mom's a nurse."

"Yes. Mom was a nurse." Marsha or Melissa or Melanie, who's also dolled up to the nines, also in black, grabs him by the elbow and steers him from the shards.

"I kept my promise, didn't I? I kept it. Jane, I kept it."

"Come on, Grandpa. We don't want to be late."

"No. Not dish time." He's back at the tiny apartment, Jane in her wedding dress. He takes the strangers' hands, lets them lead him to the big black car outside. Pretends to ignore their tears because he doesn't know how to ask about them anymore. "Definitely not dish time."

Made in the USA
Middletown, DE
24 March 2023

27600420R00125